"Kori, what is that on

As she stood at the end of the table, Brent caught her hand and held it. He was shocked to see that a gleaming diamond ring had replaced the simple gold band she used to wear.

Kori pulled away. "I'm engaged, Brent. I'm engaged to be married—to someone else."

A rush of anger rose up in Brent as he stood, facing Kori now. "That's impossible," he countered through a clenched jaw. "You can't marry someone else. . .you're already married. To me!"

"Not for long!"

ANDREA BOESHAAR was born and raised in Milwaukee, Wisconsin. Married for twenty years, she and her husband Daniel have three sons, two of whom are adults. Andrea has been writing for over thirteen years, but writing exclusively for the Christian market for six. Writing is something she loves to share, as well as, help others develop. Andrea recently quit her job to stay home, take care of her family, and write.

HEARTSONG PRESENTS

Second Time Around

Andrea Boeshaar

Heartsong Presents

For Daniel, whose love and support keeps me at the computer keyboard.

To God be the glory!

A big thank you to all my friends at St. Mary's Medical Clinic in West Allis. And special thanks to Lynn Whitney for providing me with ASCAP and PROCK information. Also, to Sally, whose advice and suggestions proved most valuable.

All scripture quotations, unless otherwise indicated, are taken from the HOLY BIBLE, NEW INTERNATIONAL VERSION®. NIV®. Copyright © 1973, 1978, 1984 by International Bible Society. Used by permission of Zondervan Publishing House. All rights reserved.

A note from the author:
I love to hear from my readers! You may correspond with me by writing: **Andrea Boeshaar**
Author Relations
PO Box 719
Uhrichsville, OH 44683

ISBN 1-57748-476-2

SECOND TIME AROUND

The Impossible Dream, lyrics by Joe Darion, music by Mitch Leigh, © 1965, used by permission, Andrew Scott Music, Helena Music Company Publishers

Cover illustration by Chris Cocozza.

prologue

The sun was just beginning to set in the smoggy Los Angeles sky when Korah Mae McDonald got off work from her second job. During the day, from seven A.M. to three P.M., Kori worked in the Medical Center's admitting department. Then, from four to nine, she worked a part-time job as a waitress.

But it will be worth it someday, Kori reminded herself. *Just as soon as Brent finishes his residency. One more month. Then he'll be a doctor. Dr. Brent McDonald.*

Kori was so proud of her husband. Proud, but exhausted! Brent had been in school, on and off, for the last fifteen years and Kori had supported him for over a decade.

She and Brent had met in college twelve years ago, back in 1981. Kori was a freshman and Brent, a junior. They married two years later when she was twenty years old and he was twenty-four. Then, after Brent was accepted to medical school, Kori abandoned her own studies for a job so Brent could continue with his education. His goals seemed more important than her business degree. Brent had a passion for medicine, just as he had a passion for everything else he did in life, and Kori couldn't deny the world the best doctor it would probably ever know.

So she worked and worked hard. Brent, too, had held various part-time jobs whenever he could; however, the bulk of the financial burden had fallen on Kori's shoulders. But she didn't mind. Brent was worth it!

Juggling her purse, tote bag, and keys, Kori unlocked the door to the apartment she and Brent shared. The small unit consisted of only a living room, kitchen, and bathroom, but Kori had done her best to make it feel homey, decorating it with her handiwork. Framed needlework, sayings and scenes, hung on walls in nearly every room. "Love Is Forever" met Kori as she entered the apartment. "Home Is Where You Hang Your Heart" was the next proclamation, hanging in the hallway near the kitchen.

However, the next sight that greeted Kori wasn't all that pleasant and it was becoming far too familiar—as were the sounds accompanying it. Brent and four of his "doctor" friends crowded the small living room, the room that also served as the bedroom once the couch was pulled out. It irritated Kori that she couldn't just relax after her long day, but she was determined to be nice. . .for Brent's sake.

"Hi, everyone," she said, forcing a smile.

The greeting was ignored, or perhaps unheard, beneath the raucous laughter.

Kori walked into the kitchen area feeling more discouraged now than tired. She had a hunch that Brent's friends didn't like her. They habitually discussed topics that were over her head, though Kori caught on to more than they realized because of her experience in the admitting department. And the other day she overheard Meg Stark refer to her as "the country bumpkin." But worse was the fact that she'd seen Brent smirk at the remark. He didn't bother to defend her where once he would have. Once she and Brent had been the best of friends; however, lately Kori felt forgotten.

With a weary sigh, she kicked off her shoes and unpacked her tote bag. A thermos, a Tupperware lunch box. Next she filled the sink and began to wash the dishes that Brent and his friends had accumulated.

I'm glad he found some supper, she mused, washing Chinese food off the plastic plates. But she couldn't help wishing that Brent would have thought to save her a bite. She was hungry since she didn't get a chance to grab anything at the diner tonight. Looking out over the counter and into the living room, Kori wished Brent would try to include her. . .the way he used to. But he didn't anymore, and things had been getting progressively worse between them in the past several months.

Kori continued to clean the kitchen until, at last, Brent's friends roused themselves and headed for the door. Kori heaved a breath of relief. Finally she could put up her tired feet and watch a little television.

"Oh, hi, Kori," one of Brent's departing buddies called. Then he added, "Bye, Kori."

"*Au revoir,* Kori," another said.

"*Arrivederci,* Kori." That was Meg's parting shot. Then she added, "Just remember, Brent, there's fifty ways to leave your lover."

His friends all chuckled.

"Shut up, you guys," Brent said irritably. Then Kori heard him mumble something about not making things easy. . .

Finally Brent closed the door on all of them.

"Mind telling me what's going on?" Kori asked warily. She could sense something. . .something very wrong.

Brent sighed, raking a hand through his straight, jet-black hair, an ancestral trait. He was part Native American and his swarthy features revealed his heritage. The other part of his makeup was Irish and his zest for life lent credence to that nationality as well. But now, as he stood before her, Kori saw a tumult of emotions cross his handsome face. Then a sort of hardness entered his mahogany-colored eyes.

"What is it, Brent?"

"I don't know," he hedged. "It's you. . .it's me. It's us." He turned away and walked into the living room, leaving Kori standing at the edge of the kitchen area.

"I think it's your friends," she said calmly. She understood him well enough to know that he was easily swayed. Every cause that came his way, Brent wanted to stand for it, fight for it. That part of his character was, in fact, the reason he had taken so long to finish med school. He was easily distracted. But Kori. . .she was his voice of reason, or so Brent told her on many occasions.

"Leave my friends out of this, Kori. They've got nothing to do with my decision—"

"What decision?"

Brent paused momentarily before turning to face her again. "I'm leaving you, Kori. Tonight. I'm moving in with Brad Henschel. I can't put it off any longer."

"You're leaving me?" she asked incredulously. "I. . .I don't understand. . .?"

"It's not too difficult," Brent replied in a patronizing tone. "A child could figure it out. I'm leaving. Period."

Kori walked slowly toward him, stunned that he could be so casual about something like their life together. "Why don't you think this over?" She reasoned. "We've been through some hard years together, but they're almost over. The best is yet to come. I suggest you stay away from your friends for a week and—"

"No," Brent said adamantly, shaking his dark head. "It's over, Kori. I. . .I just don't love you anymore."

His words cut straight to her heart, piercing it through with an unimaginable sorrow. *I just don't love you anymore.* And all she could do was watch tearfully as Brent packed his things and left their apartment.

❧

Three months later, Kori sat on one of the park benches outside the hospital where Brent now worked. He had been hired by a group of emergency physicians almost immediately after completing his residency. But that came as no surprise to Kori. Brent was the best physician she knew. What did surprise her, however, was the fact that he was determined to get a divorce. She had been so sure that he'd change his mind. . .

Looking across the hospital's front yard, Kori suspected Brent's reasons involved Meg, the "other woman." She couldn't prove it, though. Nor did she care to. There was definitely some truth to that old cliché "ignorance is bliss." Kori couldn't stand to think of Brent and Meg together. Except it made sense. Meg Stark was prettier, with her stylish, blond "bob" hair style and willowy figure. Kori, on the other hand, did what she could with her long, naturally "brassy" blond hair. She hadn't the money to spend in the professional salons. . .like Meg. And Kori's figure, though not "fat," was full. She was soft and round where Meg was straight and firm. Kori was a farm girl. Meg was a city slicker. Obviously, Brent decided he preferred the latter.

*I just don't love you anymore. . .*Kori thought those words would haunt her till the day she died!

With a breaking heart and her world crashing at her feet, Kori read Brent's latest note of instruction.

Go see Tom Sandersfeld. He's handling our divorce and taking care of the paperwork. He needs your signature.

Kori folded up the letter. She remembered Tom Sandersfeld. He and Brent had met at school a couple of years ago. Tom had been a friend—to her as well as Brent. But now he was Brent's attorney and obviously Brent's friend, not hers.

Kori sighed. She supposed she should be compliant and sign the divorce papers; however, before she signed anything, Kori wanted to talk to Brent one more time. Perhaps he would have a change of heart after all.

Still sitting on the bench, she waited patiently until he finally emerged from the hospital. She watched him walk toward the adjacent parking structure that housed his brand-new, little red sports car. Ironically, Kori thought that the new car matched Brent's new, careless lifestyle as a single emergency physician. Attracting women wouldn't be a problem if and when he tired of Meg—and the idea sent a wave of heartsickness through Kori.

"Brent!" she called just before he disappeared into the parking structure.

He stopped and she ran toward him. "What is it, Kori?"

She reached him, hoping against hope that he would change his mind and want her back.

"I got your letter," she began. She held it up so he could see. "But I. . .well, I don't want a divorce." Tears gathered in her eyes. "I love you, Brent. Can't we work this out? I'll do *anything*."

He shook his head. "Kori, there's nothing you can do. My mind is made up."

Her heart took a plunge. "But I thought we were happy together."

"That's just it, Kori, you were happy and I wasn't."

"You weren't? But I thought—"

"You thought wrong," Brent replied irritably. Then he paused and began to address her like he might a very slow child. "Look, Kori, I don't love you anymore and I want out of our marriage. Is that too much for you to comprehend?"

"No," Kori murmured, her tears threatening to choke her. "I understand more than you think. You want Meg, not me."

"Leave Meg out of this."

Kori smiled bitterly, meeting Brent's dark gaze straight on. "It's a good thing you realized how *unhappy* you were with me *after* I worked two jobs and put you through med school!"

At that Brent merely smirked. Then he turned and walked away, heading toward his new sports car.

❧

"Oh, Kori, I'm so sorry to hear about you and Brent," her older sister Clair crooned over the telephone line later that day. "Why don't you move to Wisconsin? You can live with my roommate Dana and me. What's keeping you in California?"

"My two jobs, that's what."

"You could get a job—make that *jobs* right here."

"I don't have any money. My old, beat up car won't make the trip and I can't afford airfare." Discouraged, Kori plopped down on the couch. "How's that? Three reasons right there."

"Mere technicalities," Clair replied in her usual optimistic tone. She was always outgoing and very practical, whereas Kori was serious and somewhat introspective. "I'll wire you the money."

Kori smiled, knowing her sister could afford it, too. Clair had a wonderful job with a national firm. She'd gotten transferred to Wisconsin over three years ago—and she loved it there.

"And Mom and Dad will help you. . .as much as they can, anyway." Their parents lived in a rural, little-nothing-town in Idaho. "Call them."

"I did. Dad wants me to come home."

"Oh, bother!" Clair replied, sounding like Winnie the Pooh. "You'll never have a moment's independence if you move back with Mom and Dad. Mom will mother you to death and Dad will give you an eleven o'clock curfew."

Kori laughed, but Clair was right. Their parents would always see them as girls and not grown women. Kori didn't want to go home.

"So what do you say? Wisconsin or bust!"

Kori thought it over. "But what if Brent decides to reconcile?"

"Leave him your address and phone number."

"But what if—"

"Kori, stop it. Stop building false hopes. The reality is: Brent is gone. You've got to start your own life now and what better way to do that than to move and begin all over again here in Wisconsin? Besides," Clair added, "California is too hot in the summer. Wisconsin is beautiful! Come for a few months. You'll see. And, if you don't find a job or you don't like it here, I'll pay your way home, too."

Tears gathered in Kori's eyes. "You'd do that for me, Clair?" After all these years of "doing" for Brent, it was nice that someone wanted to take care of her for a change.

Clair was laughing. "Of course I'd do that for you. Big sis to the rescue. Now, pack your bags, darlin'," she drawled, "and get yourself on the next flight out."

"Yes, ma'am," Kori replied good-naturedly. Her decision was suddenly made: she would start a brand-new life—without Brent!

one

Two and a half years later

The busy, ever-growing Westpoint Medical Clinic, in West Allis, Wisconsin, was winding down for the weekend. At five o'clock on this Friday afternoon, it was already dark outside. Doing the preliminary work, Kori had taken her last patient's blood pressure and now Dr. Ryan Carlson had gone into the exam room.

Back at her desk, Kori completed the route slips for the day. As Ryan's medical assistant, Kori had patient contact and paperwork galore, but she loved her job. Ryan had hired her two years ago as a secretary, promising to train her for the medical assistant position. In the meantime, Kori attended the area's technical college and took the courses required for the certification exam. She passed and, with Ryan's help, she was promoted to a certified MA.

Ryan Carlson was a joy to work for and the two of them got along quite well. His manner was unpretentious and amicable, even if he was somewhat of a religious fanatic.

Ryan was one of those "born-again" people and he never hesitated to tell Kori about the love of Jesus—mere words, she thought; however, Ryan's warm, friendly, and very Christian-like conduct gave her pause. In fact, she was almost envious of his new love interest, a woman by the name of Stacie Rollins whom, he said, he had met at church.

Imagine meeting someone at church, Kori thought, gazing at the picture of Jared Graham, her fiancé. He was posed on a lake pier, holding the tail of the fish he'd just caught. She had to admit the fish was something, too. The thing was nearly as long as Jared was tall, and Jared's countenance told of his pride over his catch.

Kori smiled, remembering how she and Jared had met at Clair's company picnic last summer. Jared worked for one of the affiliated divisions and he was handsome in a brawny way. He was a "man's man" who hunted, fished, bowled, played baseball, basketball. . .the list seemed never-ending. And he was rather impatient when it came to female sensibilities, but Kori tried not to mind that aspect of his personality too much.

The upside, she told herself, was that Jared would not be easily persuaded by each and every female who crossed his path. In fact, Kori doubted that he would have noticed her— except she had literally run into him at the picnic, spilling a thirty-two-ounce cola down the front of his shirt. That was when he *noticed* her, and he had obviously liked what he saw. They started talking, Kori offering to have the shirt laundered and Jared insisting it wasn't worth it. By the time the picnic was over, Jared had asked her out on a date—and they'd been seeing each other since.

Then last month he proposed marriage. Kori accepted, though she couldn't say that she actually *loved* Jared. But maybe she didn't really know what love was anymore. Since her divorce, Kori had been questioning many things— including love.

However, Jared wasn't anything like Brent. Jared was practical, sensible, and. . .stable. No more chasing one rainbow after another. Not with Jared. But that's what life had been like with Brent.

Shaking herself out of her musings, Kori went back to her route slips, but it wasn't long before her thoughts returned to Jared. She wondered if, perhaps, she shouldn't have accepted his marriage proposal. Maybe it wasn't fair, Jared being in love with her and Kori so uncertain about her feelings. Furthermore, Ryan had voiced friendly concerns, and now his misgivings were somehow causing Kori to have doubts. Why couldn't she just fall in love with Jared? Why was love such a complicated matter?

Love. It was what Kori longed for in this world. She was so incredibly lonely, even with her sister Clair and their roommate Dana around. Kori's longing for the love of someone who would cherish and protect her was like an abyss in her soul, aching to be filled. And she hoped Jared was that someone who would teach her how to fall in love again.

Kori forced her thoughts back to the present and finished her paperwork. At six o'clock, she punched out, leaving the clinic for the weekend. She walked through the darkened parking lot, heading for her 1986 Chevette.

She had bought the car for a thousand dollars from a friend of Clair's. Ryan had called it "answered prayer" since Kori was, at the time, in desperate need of transportation. The apartment she shared with Clair and Dana was in New Berlin, a western suburb just outside of Milwaukee County. However, there wasn't a handy bus route, making getting to and from work a hardship. But with a car, it was easy and, within ten minutes, Kori was pulling into the parking structure of the apartment complex in which she lived.

"Hello? Anybody home?" she called minutes later, unlocking the door and entering the apartment. When no one answered, Kori dropped her purse and took off her winter coat, hanging it up in the closet. Then she sorted through the mail that had been set on the little table in the front hallway by Dana, who habitually came home for lunch.

Claiming a few bills, Kori walked into her bedroom and put them on the desk. Next she changed from her uniform to black stirrup pants and a large sweatshirt that came to her knees.

Comfortable now, she padded through the tastefully decorated living room. Clair, whose hobby was interior design, had done it in mauves, blues, and greens, and one piece of furniture complimented the next, pulling the whole room together. But how Clair ever came to be an insurance adjuster, Kori would never know!

And then there was Dana, the beautiful, intellectual, personable banker by day and the gourmet chef by night. She said cooking helped her relax, but her delicious creations made dieting next to impossible. In fact, one of Dana's meals necessitated a good half hour on the treadmill!

Turning up the heat, Kori headed for the kitchen just as Dana Taylor burst through the front door.

"Hiya, Kori. Have a good day?" Dana's straight, blond hair hung to her shoulders, flaring slightly from the static electricity in the air, and the cold outside seemed to have turned her eyes a brighter blue.

"My day was all right. How 'bout yours?"

"Pretty good." Taking off her navy-blue wool coat, Dana walked through the apartment and met Kori in the kitchen. "Did you get my message?"

"No. What message?"

Dana laughed. "Oh, it's right here. On the counter. I meant to put it in with your mail." She handed the slip of paper to Kori. "Some guy called for you."

And that's just what the note said, too. It read: *Some guy called for you.*

Fighting the urge to laugh, Kori nodded her thanks.

"Sorry to be such a bubblehead," Dana said apologetically. "I should have asked for his name, but he said he'd call back. It wasn't Jared, either. Probably some salesman," her roommate continued as she opened the refrigerator and pulled out a can of cola. She popped the top. "Those guys always call at lunchtime or around the dinner hour." Dana sipped the soda before grinning mischievously. "You're not two-timing poor Jared, are you?"

Kori gave her a quelling look. "Me? Please! Jared is the first man I dated since coming to Wisconsin." She smiled then. "But I think Jared is a keeper."

Dana returned her smile just as the telephone rang. "I'll race you," she teased.

Both women pounced on the poor cordless phone, which had been tossed haphazardly on the sofa. But it was Dana who picked up the call.

"Oh. . .it's just you, Jared," she said, disappointed. "Yeah, she's here." Dana handed the phone to Kori.

"Come on, Dana. Smile. Your sweetheart will be the next caller."

Dana tossed her blond head. "He'd better be, if he knows what's good for him!"

Kori laughed, putting the receiver to her ear. "Hi, Jared."

"Hey, how's my best girl?" he asked jovially.

Kori was still smiling. "I'm great. Are we going out tonight?"

"Sure. My bowling team needs a scorekeeper. How 'bout it?"

"Scorekeeper?" Kori hid her disappointment. She would rather go out to dinner and a movie alone with Jared than share him with his bowling team. However, Kori knew she'd better get used to it.

She forced a smile into her voice. "Sure. Sounds good."

"Great. Afterwards we can rent a movie and go back to your place."

"All right." Things were looking up.

Jared said he'd come for her at eight and then their conversation ended. No sooner had Kori hung up the telephone, when it rang again. This time it was Tim, calling for Dana. Clair came home moments later, and the apartment was buzzing with activity.

"Zach is picking me up at seven," she sighed, looking at her wristwatch. "I have to shower and change. . .I'll never make it." She looked at Kori and smiled. "But I'll die trying!"

They laughed as Clair hurried into the back of their three-bedroom apartment, while Dana finished her conversation with her boyfriend. Then she and Kori shared a light supper, after which both women freshened up for the evening ahead.

At eight o'clock, Jared arrived. He was dressed casually in blue jeans and his red-and-white bowling league shirt. "Ready to go?" he asked. He didn't even bother removing his jacket, indicating that *he* was ready to go.

Kori nodded.

Just then, Clair clicked off the portable phone. "Plans have changed. Zach and I are staying home. . .and I'm cooking."

Kori grinned as she and Jared headed for the door. "Does Zach know what he's getting into?" she teased. "Maybe you'd better order out."

Clair gave her a pert little smile. "I am a very good cook, Korah Mae, and you know it!"

Kori winced at her given name. Only her big sister would stoop so low as to call her "Korah Mae."

Meanwhile, Jared was chuckling at them. "Well, I hope you and Zach don't mind if Kori and I come back here with rented videos."

"No, we don't mind," Clair replied. "We can watch them together. . .if you guys don't mind, that is."

"Guess I don't care," Jared said. Then he looked at Kori. "What about you, honey?"

A warm feeling flooded Kori's being at Jared's use of the endearment. "I don't care, either," she said, thinking that it really should be so easy to fall in love with him. . .

Minutes later, they left the apartment. "I've got a great idea, Kori," Jared said once they were outside. He unlocked the passenger side of his pickup truck and opened the door. "I was thinking that maybe we'd get married on a cruise ship."

"What?"

Jared closed the door before answering. Then, walking around the front of the truck, he opened the other door and climbed in behind the steering wheel.

"Yeah, these cruises are supposed to be really great," he informed her. "You go down to St. Thomas and get married by the justice of the peace."

"A cruise. . ." The idea began to grow on her. "Oh, Jared! A cruise. It's sounds so. . .romantic." *And maybe,* Kori added silently, *it'll be just the thing to make me fall in love.*

Jared looked over at her with enthusiasm shining from his eyes. "Yeah, and we could go fishing along the reef in the morning before we get married!"

Kori gazed back at him from beneath raised brows. "Fishing? On our wedding day?"

Jared shrugged. "Sure. Why not?"

Kori sighed. "Yeah, why not. . ."

"Don't you like my idea? Or don't you know how to fish?"

Kori laughed softly. "I know how. Clair and I used to fish in the little stream behind our house all the time."

"And wasn't it a thrill when you actually caught something? Now just imagine fishing along the coral reef."

"I can't wait," Kori said on a little note of sarcasm.

Jared didn't notice, however. "I can't either. This'll really be a great time." He laughed. "We'll never forget our wedding day, that's for sure—especially if we mount something we catch!"

He was as eager as a little boy and Kori softened. She wouldn't hurt him for the world. If Jared wanted to go fishing on their wedding day, that was fine with her. She was just glad that he included her in his fishing trip plans—the way Brent used to include her before he'd met his precious friends and dumped her.

"So what do you think?"

Kori brought her thoughts around to the present. "About the cruise?" She smiled. "I love the idea, Jared."

"Okay. How 'bout February?"

"A cruise in February, the same month as Valentine's Day? A cruise to St. Thomas?" Kori couldn't help a dreamy sigh. "It sounds marvelous, Jared, and the perfect thing to do in the middle of winter!"

He smiled. She smiled. And both were suddenly lost in their own, separate dreams.

two

The bowling alley was noisy, crowded, and smokey, but Kori had a relatively fun evening. She kept an accurate running score and cheered Jared on. He was, she decided, a very good bowler.

Around eleven o'clock, they left for an all-night video shop where they chose several movies. Then it was back to Kori's place to watch them.

Sitting around the television, the three couples passed a bowl of hot buttered popcorn. Dana and Tim sat together on the sofa while Kori claimed the armchair, leaving Jared, Clair, and Zach to sit on the floor. But once the movie got underway, Clair stood and motioned Kori to follow her into the kitchen area.

"What's up?"

"I wanted to wait until everyone else was occupied with the movie," Clair whispered. She smiled sympathetically. "I hate to be the one to tell you this, but Brent called tonight."

Kori raised her brows, surprised. "Brent?" At her sister's nod, she frowned. "What did he want?"

"He wants to talk to you. Said it's important. He'd like you to call him back. He's in town. Here's his telephone number."

"Here? In Wisconsin? Brent?"

Clair nodded and handed over the phone message. "He said he called around lunchtime, too."

"So that's who called," Kori murmured, glancing at the slip of paper for a good minute. She wondered what this all meant. Finally she crumpled it into a ball and tossed it into the wastebasket. *Two points!* as Jared would say.

"I won't return Brent's call," Kori said with a stubborn tilt to her chin. "I don't have anything to say to him."

"Yeah, I figured, and I told him you'd feel that way."

"And?"

"And. . .Brent said that unless you phoned him before midnight tonight, he would pick you up at eight o'clock tomorrow morning for breakfast."

"He wouldn't dare!" Kori exclaimed, horrified.

"Well, it didn't sound like a mere threat," Clair replied in her usual, calm manner.

Kori, on the other hand, gasped. "Where's that phone number?"

"I think you're too late."

Clair laughed as Kori dug through the kitchen garbage like a naughty puppy. Then, after she found the slip of paper, she had to wipe off the food particles just so she could read the phone number.

"I suppose this is what I get for being impulsive."

"I suppose," Clair replied, smiling broadly.

"This isn't funny."

"Sorry." Clair forced the smile off her face. "But I'm just dying to know what Brent wants."

"Why didn't you ask him?"

"I did. He wouldn't tell me."

Kori frowned, looking at the clock. It was 12:45.

"Like I said: I think you're too late. You didn't even get back home until 12:15."

"I'm going to call him anyhow," Kori said decisively. "Brent deserves to be awakened at this time of night. Don't you think? After what he put me through."

"You're heartless, Kori," Clair teased.

Ignoring the remark, Kori slipped into her bedroom unnoticed and dialed Brent's phone number. Her heart pounded anxiously as she listened to it ring and ring.

What could he possibly want? she wondered.

Moments later, she realized that Brent wasn't going to answer. Placing the receiver in its cradle, Kori left her bedroom and reentered the living room. She caught Clair's gaze, shook her head in silent reply, and sat back down in the arm-chair. She pondered the idea of Brent showing up here at eight o'clock in the morning.

And then she saw him in her mind's eye, his handsome, swarthy features, his dark eyes staring back at her. She heard his voice: *I just don't love you anymore. . .*and a rush of hurt-ful memories flooded her being. Then she saw the smirk on his face as he walked away, leaving her heartbroken.

Oh, Brent, what do you want? she wondered once again, only this time she had to fight down a familiar wave of heartache.

Glancing at Jared then, she told herself that Brent no longer had a hold on her. She forced herself to believe that, since she was engaged to Jared now. And, of course, she had every right to refuse to see Brent altogether. However, some-thing inside of Kori was curious—as curious as Clair's, "I'm just dying to know." After all, curiosity was a family charac-ter flaw, and Kori's mind immediately conjured up questions such as. . .What did Brent look like after two and a half years? Was he still as handsome? Did he remarry? Was it Meg? Was he still a doctor? And what was he doing in Wisconsin?

Well, maybe she'd just have to find out. Kori knew she'd be forever curious, to the point where it would drive her crazy if she didn't take the opportunity to speak with Brent one last time.

Besides, after all she'd done for him, he could at least buy her breakfast!

&

The next morning, Kori arose early, showered, and dressed. She changed clothes three times before deciding what to wear. Then, finally, coming out of her bedroom, Kori stopped short at the sight that greeted her. "What are you two doing awake at this hour?" she asked her roommates who sat non-chalantly at the dining room table sipping their coffee.

"I'll give you three guesses," Clair quipped.

Kori lifted a brow. "Snoops!"

"Bingo!" said Dana. "And we're not even ashamed of it. What do you think about that?"

Kori couldn't help a little grin as she patted the fat french braid she'd fixed in her hair this morning. It fell to the middle of her back.

Dana was looking her over. "Nice outfit. Dressing up for the ex, huh?"

"Is it too much?" Kori glanced down at the soft, loose-fitting, emerald green sweater that hung over a full denim skirt, blue tights and brown, leather ankle boots.

"You look like you just stepped out of a Laura Ingalls Wilder book," Clair remarked. "All you need is the bonnet."

"Oh, no. . .I'll go change."

"Don't change. You look fine!" Dana declared. "Don't listen to Clair. What does she know about fashion? Besides, Brent will be here—"

The buzzer sounded.

"—any second," Dana finished.

They all looked at each other.

"Well, one of us should get the door," Clair said.

"I will!"

Dana ran for it like a little girl at a birthday party and Clair rolled her eyes while Kori stood by nervously.

"Are you sure I look all right?"

Clair nodded. "Really, Kori, you look great. I was just teasing."

"Nice to meet you," they heard Brent say after Dana buzzed him up from the lobby and introduced herself. "I'm Brent McDonald. Is Kori here?"

"Yes. She's expecting you. Come on in." A moment of silence. "Have a seat. I'll get her."

Kori and Clair waited as their friend walked from the living room, through the dining area, and into the small alcove by the bedrooms where they now stood.

"Are you guys hiding?" Dana whispered.

"Yes," Kori replied, having second thoughts about the meeting now that she'd heard Brent's voice.

"He seems very polite," Dana remarked "And he's a fine-looking man. You've got good taste in men, Kori."

She groaned. "I think I'd better change."

Clair shook her head, then looked at Dana. "You take one arm, I'll take the other."

"No, no. . ." Quietly, Kori slapped at their hands. "We're all being silly, aren't we? I mean, this is just Brent. My ex-husband. There's nothing between us anymore. He means nothing to me. He's just someone that I used to know."

"Who are you trying to convince?" Clair asked. "Dana and me—or yourself?"

Kori refused to even acknowledge such a question, and lifting a determined chin, she pushed past her roommates and marched into the living room.

Brent was sitting on the sofa, looking calm and relaxed. He wore navy-blue cotton slacks and a red, blue, and green plaid cotton shirt. He appeared amazingly the same, his thick dark hair parted to one side, except that he now wore glasses. They were a classic style and made him look sophisticated.

"Hello, Brent," Kori said uncertainly.

He snapped to attention and stood at the sound of her voice. "Hi, Kori."

She watched as he looked her over and a feeling of self-consciousness enveloped her. Kori knew she wasn't a strikingly attractive woman. In fact, she doubted that she had changed much from the day he'd left her.

But that was when Brent surprised her. "You're as lovely as ever," he said, walking toward her and smiling. "It's good to see you again."

An instant later, she was in his arms for a quick embrace, after which Brent pressed a soft kiss on her mouth, leaving Kori's senses reeling.

She never saw it coming. . .but her roommates had! They stood by grinning like two Cheshire cats.

Kori turned to them, her face flaming with embarrassment over her obvious reaction to Brent's kiss. He shouldn't have affected her like this—but he had!

"You met Dana, already, Brent," she managed to mutter. "Do you remember my sister, Clair?"

"Of course. Hi, Clair." He held out his hand and she took it. Then Brent kissed her cheek.

"So. . .are you still an ER doctor?" Clair asked.

Brent nodded. "I work for the same emergency physicians' group. We service several hospitals around the Los Angeles area. But I've taken a leave of absence until the end of January."

"A leave of absence?" Clair echoed.

Brent flashed her a charming smile. "Kori can tell you all about it after our, uh, breakfast meeting this morning." He turned to her. "Shall we go?"

Kori wanted to protest. After all, what would Jared say if he saw her dining with her ex-husband? Of course, he was probably deer hunting already. He and his friend Bob had had plans to leave for the north woods early this morning.

Clair, good sister that she was, brought over her coat and Brent helped her into it. Then, before Kori could think of an excuse not to go, they were gone.

"My truck is parked up the street," Brent said as they walked along the sidewalk.

"Your truck? What happened to your sports car?"

Brent shrugged, looking chagrined. "I sold it. It really wasn't me, I guess."

Kori didn't reply as she stepped in time with his strides. The day was cold and gloomy and the trees were bare, their limbs resembling gnarled fingers. She put her gloved hands into her coat pockets to stave off the chill.

"Why are you taking me to breakfast, Brent?" Kori couldn't help but ask.

He paused before answering. "I need to speak with you about something very important."

"Oh?" She gave him a suspicious look. "What is it?"

"Let's discuss it over breakfast. That seems much more appealing than out in this cold and on the sidewalk." He smiled disarmingly. "But what I want to talk to you about is only a part of the reason I'm here. It's the biggest part, but there is something else."

"And that is?"

"Remember Mark Henley?"

Kori thought for a moment and then nodded. "From school. . .blond, blue eyes. . .nice guy."

"That's him." Brent smiled again. "Well, he's getting married next month and I'm in the wedding."

"The wedding is here? In Wisconsin?"

Brent nodded. "Actually, it's in Menomonee Falls, not too far from here."

"I see." Kori knew where it was. The community was just another suburb of Waukesha County, similar to New Berlin where she lived.

"Mark took a job as a business consultant for a large firm in Menomonee Falls," Brent explained. "There he met up with his high school sweetheart and now he's finally going to marry her."

"How nice," Kori replied for lack of a better response. But she remembered Mark, all right. He was handsome, hard-working, and smiled easily. And he was always working on that old car of his.

"Here's my truck."

Kori snapped out of her musings and stared at the handsome Jeep Cherokee 4 X 4. It was a four-door utility vehicle in a deep forest green. Impressive, but hardly flashy and pretentious like the sports car.

Brent unlocked the door and Kori climbed in. She noticed that the vehicle was loaded with every feature imaginable, a far cry from Jared's dusty but faithful pickup truck.

"You travel in style," she commented as Brent slid in behind the steering wheel. "I'm impressed."

"Thanks. I bought this 4 X 4 about eighteen months ago."

"Business must be booming. First a sports car and now this."

Brent shrugged. "Business isn't too bad."

"Hmm. . .well, in that case, maybe I should sue you for about fifty thousand bucks," Kori said on a sarcastic note. "That's the least I invested in you. I think I ought to get it back."

"Kori, if you want fifty thousand bucks, I'll give it to you." Brent gave her a sideways glance. "My dad left me a good chunk of money."

"Oh?" She lifted a curious brow.

"You're aware that he died, aren't you? Wait, no, never mind. I know my mother wrote and told you. And I saw the sympathy card you sent our family. That was thoughtful, Kori."

She shrugged. She had always been fond of her in-laws, though they hadn't corresponded much since the divorce.

"Well, anyway," Brent continued, pulling away from the curb and driving toward Mayfair Road, "Dad had been buying stock in the factory for which he worked, and its value doubled over the years. Then it doubled again. Dad wasn't even aware of his wealth until about three months before he died. He discovered it while settling his business affairs." Brent cleared his throat. "He went to see Tom Sandersfeld. Remember him?"

"Sure," Kori said flatly. "He's that *friend* of yours who took care of our divorce."

"Ah. . .yeah, right." Brent shot her a guilty-looking grin.

"Oh, I get it," Kori stated knowingly. "Since you inherited all this money, you want to settle with me so I won't come back and sue you later. Right?"

"No, Kori, I—"

She laughed, a bitter note to her own ears, yet she was sure that had to be the reason for this little "breakfast meeting," as Brent had called it. "No wonder you'd hand over fifty thousand dollars without batting an eyelash," she said. "It's probably a drop in the bucket to you now."

Brent shook his head as Kori folded her arms and raised a stubborn chin. "Well, I've got news for you, Brent," she continued. "I'm very happy with the life I've managed to rebuild after our divorce. I don't want your money. Any of it!"

"You know, I probably should have considered the money aspect, but, really, Kori, I didn't. That you would go after my inheritance never occurred to me. In fact, I'm willing to share it with you." He clicked on his turn signal and pulled off the road.

She narrowed her gaze suspiciously. "Why?"

"Well. . .because. . ." Brent gave her a wavering glance. "Say, would you mind if we ate breakfast before discussing this?"

"Before discussing what?"

"What I need to discuss with you, that's what."

Kori had to grin at the ridiculousness of his reply. Then she softened. "No, I guess I don't mind, seeing as we're already in the parking lot of the Denny's restaurant."

"This place okay with you?"

"Sure, except I thought we would be dining in elegance, now that you're a millionaire."

Brent laughed. "Hardly, Kori. I'm no millionaire, even though Dad was. He left each of us children two hundred and fifty thousand dollars—he left Mom more, of course. But if I tried hard enough, I could probably blow my entire inheritance in a year."

"I could do it in half that time," Kori retorted.

Brent laughed once more and opened the door. "Let's eat. I'm starved!"

Walking beside him into the restaurant, Kori couldn't begin to fathom what was on his mind.

three

Kori and Brent entered the restaurant and were seated by the hostess. They both ordered cups of coffee, which arrived almost immediately. Then they gazed at the menus until their waitress appeared.

"So what are you doing these days?" Brent asked after their orders were taken.

"I'm a medical assistant."

"Really?" He smiled broadly. "I guess I shouldn't be surprised, considering your medical background. I'll bet you're a wonderful MA."

Kori was somewhat taken aback by the compliment. *He must want something awfully badly,* she decided. *He sure is being nice.*

Kori looked at him from over her coffee cup. "What about you?" she couldn't help but ask. "Did you remarry?"

Brent shook his head.

"Oh, that's interesting. I had imagined that you married Meg."

"Meg?" Brent pulled his chin back in surprise, but then a softness entered his eyes. "I'll admit to having a brief attraction to her, but nothing ever happened between Meg and me. Honest, Kori. We dated a couple times after you left California, but she just wasn't my. . .type."

"Kind of like your sports car, huh?"

He shrugged, but Kori knew she was right. When Brent got tired of something, or *someone,* he tossed it aside and pursued his next avenue of interest.

"You know, Kori," Brent said, tapping the zipped-up leather-bound book he'd brought into the restaurant with him—*some day planner,* Kori thought. "I felt so empty inside for years and

28

I thought that if I was single again I'd be satisfied with life. But I wasn't. Next I thought that once I had a successful medical career I'd be satisfied. But, again, I wasn't. It seemed there was a hollowness in my soul that couldn't be filled.

"Then my father got sick and that really affected me. I wanted to be the one to help him, but I couldn't. There I was, a doctor who could save lives in the emergency room but who couldn't save his own father from terminal cancer." Brent paused. "My mortality hit me between the eyes."

Kori stared into her coffee cup. "I'm sorry, Brent. I know you loved your father very much."

He nodded. "Well, the good that came out of my dad's illness is tremendous. Miraculous, really!" Brent unzipped the leather-covered book. "Mark Henley came to visit when he found out that Dad was dying, and he showed me from the Bible how I could be saved—he showed Dad as well."

Kori's eyes grew large. "That's a. . .a Bible!"

Brent nodded.

"I thought you were carrying around your planner." She narrowed her gaze. "A Bible, Brent?"

"I'm a born-again Christian, Kori."

She laughed. "Good grief! Now I've heard everything!" She laughed once more. "Well, at least your Christianity might keep you out of trouble for awhile."

Brent gave her a curious look. "What do you mean?"

"Oh, the doctor I work for is a 'born-again' too and he seems to spend a lot of his free time in church." Kori grinned. "Can't get into trouble if you're in church all the time."

Brent smiled. "Has this doctor shared God's plan of salvation with you?"

"All the time. But I'm just not convinced. I guess Bible Christianity sounds like everything else I've experienced. I mean, I remember when you were into discovering your Native American heritage. We even went to a couple of powwows. But that got old, so you decided to be a naturalist. Remember that? We couldn't eat anything that had chemicals in it. . .

except I'll admit to sneaking a Twinkie every now and then."

Brent chuckled softly.

"And then, after you got tired of being *au natural,*" she said on a facetious note, "you got into the whole environmental thing. Then it was saving the animals."

"And now I'm into saving souls. That is, I'm into sharing the Good News of salvation."

Again, Kori shrugged. "For now. It'll be something else later."

Brent shook his head. "No. It won't. Now that I've got God in my life, I don't need all those other things—even though they are important. But they can't save like Christ can. And that's what I was missing. You see, Kori, all those years, I was searching for the Truth."

And at what price you finally found it, Kori answered inwardly. *I lost my heart and you found God.*

Brent was sipping his coffee and watching her curiously. "What about you, Kori?"

"Oh, I've got my truth," she replied tersely. "I took a little bit of everything we were into while we were married and I rolled it into one. So I guess you could say that I believe in a little bit of everything."

Brent accepted the answer. . .for now. He had no choice. Only God could change Kori's heart—like He had his own.

Brent lifted his eyes from his coffee cup to consider her as she sat across the table from him. *Lord, I was so neglectful of her,* he thought, gazing at Kori's beautiful golden-blond hair. Her hair was, in fact, the very thing which had first attracted him. Like a beacon, it had signaled him from across the lecture hall at UCLA. Brent had instantly known that he had to meet the woman whose hair was the color of spun gold. Then, after he had finally gotten up the nerve to ask Kori out on what was their first date, she had looked up at him with eyes so pale green they were almost transparent. From that moment on, Brent knew he was doomed. It was love at first sight for him, just like in the books.

Years later, after they were married, Kori had given up her dreams so he could attend medical school, and she never complained. She just gave of herself freely, never expecting anything in return. Now that was love! But Brent just hadn't seen it. He'd been so blind. And he had never been able to fill the void that leaving Kori had put in his heart. She had been his friend, his confidant—his one true love, and more than anything, Brent wanted her back! He only hoped the news he had for her wouldn't come as too much of a shock.

Breakfast arrived, Kori having ordered the "Grand Slam" special and Brent a steak and eggs dish.

"Would you mind if I pray before we begin eating?" he asked.

Kori shrugged. "Sure. Go ahead." And she even bowed her head while Brent asked God's blessing on their food.

"I'm starved," Brent remarked, picking up his fork.

Kori shook her head at him. "I never thought I'd see the day when you'd be eating meat! You! Mr. Vegetarian Animal Lover!"

Brent grinned. "I don't eat a lot of it. Too much red meat isn't good for the heart."

"Oh, right, Dr. McDonald. Excuse me." Kori laughed softly and then began eating her breakfast.

A few moments of silence passed between them as they ate.

"Mom sends her love," Brent told her, salting his eggs.

Kori watched him in a mixture of amusement and disbelief. Dr. Health Food salting his eggs? Amazing!

Brent looked at her expectantly then, and she realized he was waiting for a reply. "Oh, yes. . .please tell your mother that I say hello. How is she doing since your dad's death?"

"Remarkably well. She's moving as we speak. Into a condo that's bigger than the house I grew up in!"

"She sold the house?"

"Yep. About a month ago."

"Oh." Kori mulled over the news as she took a bite of toast. She was happy for her mother-in-law, but thought it was sort of sad that she sold the family home for a condo. Then, again, things just didn't seem to mean anything to people anymore.

"Mom needed the room," Brent explained as if divining her thoughts. "She baby-sits for my nieces and nephews on a regular basis. Besides, maintaining a two-story house and a yard was too much for her."

Kori nodded. She couldn't argue with that reasoning.

"But as sorry as Mom was to sell the house with all its memories," Brent continued, "she's excited to move into her condominium. There she'll begin a new era of her life."

"And just like that, she'll forget about your father? Doesn't she miss him? Isn't she lonely now without him?"

"Hardly lonely with all her grandchildren to keep her company," Brent replied with a broad smile. "But, yes, Mom misses Dad very much. So do I."

"Oh, Brent, I'm sorry. It must have been terribly painful for you to watch your dad die that way."

"Thanks, Kori. You always were a very compassionate woman."

Another compliment, huh? Kori couldn't help but wonder what that meant. However, it wasn't like Brent never used to compliment her. He did. Often. Up until about their last six months of marriage, anyhow.

Several pensive moments passed and then Kori asked, "So, Brent, did you come to Wisconsin with the intention of saving my soul? That and Mark Henley's wedding?"

"Not really," he replied honestly, "but I did come to Wisconsin for you—mainly for you."

"For me? What do you mean?"

Brent chewed the last of his meal, wondering how to explain.

Then suddenly Kori pushed her plate off to the side. "Look, Brent," she said, "if you're on some kind of mission here, forget it and go home. I'll be honest. I've got my own life now and it doesn't include you."

Brent, too, pushed his plate away before wiping his mouth with his napkin. "Kori," he began, "I'm afraid your life includes me more than you think."

"Oh?"

She had a sudden frown on her face and it saddened Brent to see it there. But what did he expect?

"Kori, let me preface what I need to tell you by saying first that I'm sorry I hurt you." He paused. "I'm more sorry than you'll ever know. I deeply regret the pain I caused you."

Kori gave him a knowing smile. "I get it. You've reconciled with God and you think you have to beg my forgiveness. Taking me to breakfast is like. . .penance. Right?"

Brent shook his head. "I need your forgiveness. That's true, but—"

"But nothing. I forgive you, Brent, so you can now go back to California and your medical career with a clear conscience."

"Please don't be flippant about this, Kori. This is serious business."

Again, that frown. "What is?"

Brent drew a long breath. "Well, you remember Tom Sandersfeld. . ."

"You asked me that already," Kori said impatiently. "Yes, I remember him."

"Okay. Well, when I went to see him about getting a divorce, he told me that if you didn't contest it and you signed the papers—which you did—that I wouldn't even have to show up in court. It was basically a done deal. Tom said he'd take care of everything.

"But then he had a streak of bad luck. He was arrested several times for driving while intoxicated, which eventually led to his suspension from the bar. He couldn't practice law for a whole year; however, by the time my father and I went to see him, Tom had cleaned up his act and was back practicing law. Except it came up that. . .well. . ."

"Yes?"

Brent took off his glasses and rubbed the bridge of his nose. He hadn't slept well last night anticipating this very conversation—even with the telephone unplugged. He had figured Kori would try to call him and refuse to see him. But what Brent had to tell her needed to be said.

"Kori, Tom Sandersfeld never filed our divorce papers before his suspension, and he kind of forgot about it. I only found out when I went to his office with Dad that one day. I just happened to question Tom about the divorce, seeing as he never sent me a bill."

For several long moments, Kori just stared at him. Finally, she blinked, looking utterly confused. "What are you telling me, Brent?"

He licked his suddenly parched lips and forced a smile. "I'm telling you that we're still married, Kori," he said. "You're still my wife."

Her hazel eyes grew wide. "What!" At her exclamation, several heads turned at neighboring tables and Kori's color heightened. She lowered her voice. "How could you have let this happen?"

"Kori, I thought Tom had taken care of everything—just as he said."

"Oh, my!" Kori turned ashen. "You mean we're still m–married?"

Brent nodded silently, allowing the news to sink in. Then, as he watched, Kori's expression went from shocked to sensible.

"Okay, we won't panic," she told him. "We'll just. . .fix it. We can file again. . .or have you already?" She smacked her palm to her forehead. "Oh, now I understand what this is all about. You need me to sign another set of divorce papers— and something excluding me from your inheritance." She nodded as though she had it all figured out. "Fine, Brent. Hand 'em over. I'll sign whatever you want."

If the situation weren't quite so desperate, Brent would have laughed out loud. Her reaction was that comical! However,

Kori seemed shaken and. . .and even somewhat eager to have him out of her life by way of a divorce.

Then, again, what did he expect?

"Kori, what you don't understand is, I've changed my mind," he said bluntly. "I don't want a divorce anymore."

Her jaw dropped slightly. "You don't want a divorce?" She shook her head as if in disbelief. "Well, it's a little late for that, don't you think? Or didn't you think, Brent?"

"I've thought a lot about this situation, prayed about it, too, and my mind's made up. I want you back, Kori."

She gaped at him. "You've got to be kidding."

Brent shook his head. "It's no joke, Kori."

"But your mind was made up two and a half years ago when you filed for divorce. Remember? You said you didn't love me anymore. Is it coming back to you now?"

"Kori, two and a half years ago, I didn't know what love was. I was totally absorbed with myself. But I was the reason for my own unhappiness. It was never you."

Kori, however, was shaking her head. "You can't just devastate someone and then change your mind. I won't hear another word about it!"

"Kori, please!" Brent felt like his heart had somehow leapt into his throat, except he knew that was medically impossible. "Look, I've made some terrible mistakes and I've hurt you beyond imagination. I'm ashamed of myself for ever leaving you. . .but that was before God got ahold of my heart. I'm a different man now—a better one, I hope."

"Leave God out of this, Brent," she warned him, blinking back the tears.

Seeing them nearly broke his heart, but Brent was not deterred. "I can't leave God out of this. . .or any part of my life. It's because of God's mercy and grace that I'm a new man today."

"Right. And I'm Christie Brinkley." Kori scooted out of the booth.

And that's when Brent saw it. The ring on her left hand.

"Kori, what is that on your finger?"

As she stood at the end of the table, Brent caught her hand and held it. He was shocked to see that a gleaming diamond ring had replaced the simple gold band she used to wear.

Kori pulled away. "I'm engaged, Brent. I'm engaged to be married—to someone else."

A rush of anger rose up in Brent as he stood, facing Kori now. "That's impossible," he countered through a clenched jaw. "You can't marry someone else. . .you're already married. To me!"

"Not for long!"

With that, she turned on her heel and marched out of the restaurant, leaving Brent to flag down their waitress, request the bill, leave a tip, and pay for their meal before he could follow her out.

When he finally left the restaurant, Kori was nowhere to be found.

four

Standing inside the gas station across the street from the restaurant, Kori telephoned Clair to come and get her.

"Things didn't go so well, huh?" her sister asked as Kori climbed into the car.

"We're still married!" she blurted.

"What?" Clair's eyes grew wide. "You and Brent? Still married? You've got to be kidding!"

"My words exactly." Kori leaned her head back against the seat rest. "And I wish I were kidding. I wish Brent were kidding."

Clair pulled out of the gas station, heading for home.

"And the worst of it is," Kori added, "Brent doesn't want a divorce anymore. He said he changed his mind!"

Clair looked at her with clouds of disbelief in her eyes. "Well, that's not very nice!"

"Not nice? It's wicked!" Kori paused, collecting her thoughts. "It was so hard to adjust to not having Brent in my life and, now that it's finally happened, he says he's changed his mind! How could he do this to me?"

"Does he know about Jared?"

"Sort of." Kori turned to look at her sister. "I told him that I was engaged." She let out a moan. "I'm engaged to Jared but I'm married to Brent!"

Clair chuckled softly, but quickly apologized for finding anything amusing about the situation.

Finally she reached over and gave Kori's hand a squeeze. "C'mon. Cheer up, little sister," she said, pulling the car into the parking structure. "We'll bake some chocolate chip cookies this afternoon, go shopping tomorrow, and suddenly you'll see things from a different perspective."

Kori had her doubts.

"Really," Clair told her, earnestly now, "this isn't all that bad. A trip to the lawyer's office Monday morning will take care of everything. Just go ahead and file again, Kori. That's all. And I know just the person to help you, too. Tamara Mills. She's an attorney friend of mine."

"But what if Brent—"

"Stop, Kori. You can 'what if' yourself till you're purple. Just quit moping and go see an attorney."

Kori thought it over and then nodded. Perhaps she was over-reacting. There had to be a way out of this. Clair was right.

They walked through the glass-encased, well-decorated lobby and took the elevator to the second floor. Entering their apartment, Dana immediately insisted upon being informed about Kori's breakfast with "the ex."

"Okay, so let me get this straight," she said after hearing the story. "You thought you were divorced from Brent, but you're really married to him. . .but you're engaged to Jared, only Brent doesn't want a divorce anymore. And he inherited a quarter of a million dollars. . .?"

Kori collapsed into one of the armchairs. "That's about the size of it, Dana."

"Wow," she said, looking impressed. "This is even better than *Days of Our Lives!*"

Kori laughed. She couldn't help it. "My life—the soap opera. Oh, and did I tell you that Brent is a born-again Christian?"

Clair didn't look a bit surprised. "This too shall pass," she quipped. "He's been everything else."

Kori agreed. "And just like before, Brent will change his mind about marriage—just like he changed his mind about a divorce."

The buzzer sounded and Clair went to answer it.

"Hi, it's Brent," came the voice through the intercom. "I just wanted to make sure Kori got home all right."

"She's home safe and sound. Thanks." With that, Clair

released the TALK button and walked away from the front door. "You know," she said, reentering the living room, "I've got to give the guy a little credit for that one; it was very thoughtful of him to check on you, Kori."

"Yes, I suppose it was," she murmured.

But then the more Kori thought about it, the more amazing it seemed. In all the time they'd been together, Brent had never gone out of his way for her. He'd let her walk to work or take the bus while he drove their wreck of a car. He'd let her stay home and search the cupboards for supper while he ate out with his friends—on *her* paychecks. And if they argued, and if she walked away, he'd always let her go. That Brent came to see if she'd made it home all right was truly remarkable!

Finally, Kori could deny it no longer. It *was* a different Brent with whom she'd had breakfast this morning. But whoever he was now, Kori had no intention of staying married to him!

❧

Engaged! Brent tossed his car keys onto the marble-top buffet in the dining room of his rented, furnished apartment. *How could she be engaged?* He paused, deep in thought. *How could she not be? She's beautiful—more beautiful than I remembered.*

Walking into the living room, he collapsed into a large stuffed armchair. In his mind, he replayed the breakfast meeting with Kori and discouragement settled in. He had lost her for sure. Forever. Kori was going to marry someone else.

Yes, but does she love him? his heart seemed to counter in reply. *Does she love him. . .the way she loved me?*

Somehow, Brent didn't think so. He had seen something in Kori's eyes this morning when he'd kissed her hello. It was, in fact, the same "something" Brent had felt in his heart. He still loved her. He'd never stopped. He'd just been. . .confused.

And I'm willing to bet Kori still loves me, too.

Brent suddenly felt hopeful again.

és

"What do you mean, you're not going out tonight?" Clair asked. "It's Saturday night!"

Sitting on the couch with her cross-stitch in her lap, Kori shrugged. "Jared went deer hunting this morning and won't be back until tomorrow night. Besides, I'm tired."

Clair sat down next to her on the couch. "Are you having second thoughts about Brent?"

Kori shook her head.

"About Jared?"

This time, Kori shrugged. "Sometimes." Lifting her gaze from what would be her parents' Christmas gift this year, she looked at Clair. "Jared told me last night that he wants to get married in February. In St. Thomas while we're on a cruise." Kori momentarily fretted over her lower lip. "But what is Jared going to say when he finds out I'm still married to Brent?"

Clair gave her a sympathetic shrug.

"On the other hand, maybe it's best. February will come awfully fast, and I don't know if I'm really ready to marry Jared. Sometimes I wonder if I really know him. He thinks so differently from the way I do. But he is nice and I believe he wants a home and family. . .just like I do."

"But is that a good enough reason for getting married? What about love, Kori?"

She winced at the same words Ryan had spoken to her weeks earlier. "I guess that's one more reason for waiting." She gave her sister a hopeful glance. "But, in time, I know I'll come to love Jared."

"Do you really think so—even after you consider the way Brent kissed you this morning?"

Kori shifted uncomfortably. "Oh, all right. I'll admit to. . .to responding to Brent's kiss. But he caught me off guard. That's all. Besides, Brent has a passionate nature. Jared is just more. . . practical."

"Forget practical, Kori. Jared is shallow and immature."

"How can you say such a thing?"

"Because it's true." She sighed and Kori knew that the last thing Clair wanted to do was insult anyone, particularly Jared. She was just being an older sister and Kori, for the most part, appreciated it.

"Look, I know you, Kori, and I think you'll grow tired of life with Jared because you won't really be living. You'll be *existing*. . .while Jared hunts, fishes, bowls, and shoots darts."

"There's nothing wrong with what Jared does for fun."

"No, but that's *all* he does and nothing is meaningful."

"Oh, Clair, you're mistaken. Life with Jared means stability, and I'll gladly welcome that *existence* after all the turbulence I lived through with Brent!"

"Okay. It's your life."

Kori smiled gratefully. "Yes, it is, but thanks anyway."

"And, as for tonight, you can come along with Zach and me if you want. We're going to his sister's birthday party."

Kori shook her head. "I appreciate the invitation, but I'm going to finish this stitching project for Mom and Dad. I've been so busy, it'll be nice to just spend a quiet evening at home. Besides, Christmas is only about five weeks away."

Clair waved off the statement. "I'll start thinking about Christmas after I get past Thanksgiving," she said, rising from the couch.

Then she headed for the bathroom, announcing her turn in the shower and Kori smiled in her wake.

⁂

At six o'clock the buzzer sounded and Dana came running into the living room in her bathrobe. "That can't possibly be Tim!" she cried. Her hair was in curlers and she was just applying her makeup. "He said he wouldn't pick me up until seven!"

Laughing, Kori strode from the kitchen where she'd been creating supper. "Don't worry. I'll get it. I'll tell him to sit in the lobby, relax, and you'll be down shortly."

Dana replied with a grateful nod.

"Kori? Is that you?" came the all-too-familiar voice through the intercom. "It's Brent. I need to speak with you. It's important and it won't wait."

"Oh, great," Kori muttered. She turned to Dana. "Looks like you're off the hook. Go finish getting ready for your date."

"Well, you can't buzz Brent up here," Dana complained. "I'm not dressed and neither is Clair. And you know how our stuff is, like, all over the apartment!"

Grudgingly, Kori nodded. "Brent? I'll be right down," she said into the intercom. "We can talk in the lobby."

Releasing the TALK button, Kori grabbed her keys and left the apartment. In the lobby, she opened the outer door for Brent.

"Sorry, but this will have to do," she explained. "My sister and Dana are going out tonight and they're dressing."

"Are you going out tonight, too?" Brent asked.

Kori was momentarily surprised by the question. "That's really none of your business," she replied curtly.

A muscle appeared to work in Brent's jaw, but he said nothing more on the subject.

Kori led him through the warm, well-lit lobby to a place where six bright, floral-upholstered love seats were scattered about. No one else was in the area, so she and Brent could get comfortable and speak freely.

"What's up?" Kori asked, settling into one of the love seats. Brent sat down beside her and there suddenly seemed to be little space between them.

He leaned forward, his forearms resting on his knees. He was momentarily pensive, before sitting back and giving Kori a direct look. "It's about your fiancé. . ."

Kori lifted surprised brows. "Jared? What about him?"

"Jared?" Slowly, Brent shook his head. "Kori, I just can't imagine you engaged to a *Jared*."

Kori folded her arms and sighed wearily. "Brent, what do you want?"

"Look at me, Kori."

She did.

"I want you to tell me that you love *Jared* more than you ever loved me."

Something undefined tugged at her heartstrings and Kori was suddenly at a loss for words. But perhaps it was looking into Brent's dark, passionate eyes that caused her hesitation, caused her to remember. . .his kisses, his embraces, the sweet words he used to whisper in her ear. . .

At last she concluded Brent's request was impossible. Kori would never love anyone as much as she once loved Brent. However, the key word was "once," because her love for him was no more!

"Brent, you and Jared are two very different men," she tried to explain. "And I may look the same physically, but the person I am with Jared is very different from who I was when you and I were married."

"*Are* married," Brent corrected her. "And you're not answering my question. Do you love him more than me?"

Kori wanted to hurl a "Yes!" into Brent's handsome face, but the word wouldn't take form.

She stood, turning her back on him, unable to look into his dark, probing gaze another moment. "I'm going to marry Jared," she finally said with much more determination than she'd ever felt. "What does that tell you?"

Brent rose and stood behind her. Taking hold of her elbow, he turned her back around to face him.

"Jared wants a family," Kori blurted. "I want children. I want a home. And Jared is a decent man. He's got a good job—one he's been faithful to for almost fifteen years! That means a lot to me. . .stability, and Jared is a very stable man!"

"Those are fine attributes," Brent said, taking her by the shoulders and giving her a mild shake. "But do you love him more than me?"

Kori tried to twist out of his grasp, but Brent only tightened his hold. "Let go of me!" she cried in the heat of indignation. "And how can you talk to me about love after the way you hurt me? I should hate you!"

"Do you?"

Kori paused. "I. . .I don't know. . ." She heaved a sigh as tears stung the backs of her eyes. "For months after you left, after you told me you didn't love me anymore, I would lay awake at night wishing upon wish that you'd want me back. Here in Wisconsin, hundreds of miles from where you were in California, I'd wish and wish that you'd call me and say it was all a mistake. But you never did."

She saw a look of guilt and remorse cloud his dark eyes and it took all her will to press on. "Finally, I had a choice to make. I could either let my depression over our divorce make me crazy, or I could get on with my life. I chose the latter. It was so hard, Brent, but I did it. I moved on. I went to school, got a job, and found someone to love me and give me all the things that you were too selfish to give."

Again, Kori struggled out of Brent's hold but, this time, she was successful. "Go back to California," she pleaded. "Leave me alone. You can have any woman you want, but I just want to be happy. . .with Jared."

A look so pained and miserable crossed Brent's face that Kori almost relented. Almost.

Brent, however, seemed to have been rendered speechless, so Kori took his hand and led him toward the outside door. "Good night," she said softly. She swung the heavy wooden, glass-paned door open wide, leaning her back up against it. But Brent just stood there, looking like a lost boy.

Finally, he turned to her. "Kori, I'm so sorry for hurting you. It will never happen again."

"You're right," she said with a tight smile. "It won't happen again because I'm going to marry Jared and I don't think he's capable of hurting me like you did."

"So my apology means nothing?"

"Your apology is too late."

Brent narrowed his gaze and any benevolence he might have displayed before seemed to evaporate before her very eyes. "Listen, Kori," he said, "it'll be over my dead body that you marry Jared. . .or anyone else!"

She gave out a little gasp of surprise at his vehemence.

"And if I have to use every dollar of my inheritance," he continued, "and every cent I ever earn, I'm going to fight this divorce."

"Brent! Didn't you hear anything I just said?"

The question, however, fell on deaf ears as Brent stormed from the apartment building.

Watching him go, Kori's heart filled with rekindled anger. *The audacity of that man! What arrogance!*

Then, pushing the button for the elevator, Kori decided that Brent really hadn't changed all that much. He still demanded his own way. He wanted what he wanted despite the cost to anyone else.

Back inside the apartment, things were chaotic. Clair was on the telephone with Zach, replanning their evening, and Dana was madly searching for her gold hoop earrings. Ignoring the goings-on around her, Kori reclaimed her place on the sofa and resumed her stitching. And the angrier she got with Brent, the faster her needle went, in and out, in and out. She'd have this piece done in no time!

But when Dana left with her date and after Clair was gone with Zach, an old ache called loneliness bore down on Kori until she hurt all over. There were times, such as these, that Kori felt like she was the only one in the whole world. Suddenly she found herself wishing that Jared would phone. Hearing his voice would be such a comfort. To know that he took time from deer hunting with his friends to think of her would mean so much. To hear him say, "I love you" would erase Brent's words of love—not that Kori believed them. Brent didn't know what love was. Then again, neither did she. But Jared would show her, with kindness and patience, and one day she would return his love fully because she would finally understand its true meaning.

Oh, if only you'd phone, Jared, she wished.

But he never did.

five

Brent paced the living room in front of the overstuffed, plaid sofa, until finally Mark Henley cleared his throat. "You're going to wear out the carpet, Brent," he teased. "Then Mr. and Mrs. Bakersfield aren't going to be very pleased with me for recommending you as sublessee."

Brent paused. "I messed up, Mark. I totally messed up. I threatened her." He shook his head. "I can't believe I did that. I mean, what right do I have, barging into Kori's life after two years and threatening her? Some Christian I am!"

"Oh, don't beat yourself up. Christians aren't perfect. . . and you haven't been a Christian all that long, either." Mark gave him a patient smile. "So you make amends by calling up Kori and apologizing. Right?"

Nodding, Brent collapsed into a nearby armchair. "I'll apologize—except I don't want a divorce. I want a second chance."

Mark seemed thoughtful for several long moments. "Why don't you try being her friend for awhile, Brent? Then you can ask for a second chance at the husband role."

"And I should just let her file for divorce and watch her proceed merrily along in her engagement to. . .*Jared?*" Brent snorted in disgust and then couldn't help but wonder how he'd stack up beside the "other man" in Kori's life.

Mark just shrugged. "Look at it this way. Divorces take awhile, don't they? Perhaps that will buy you time."

This time Brent shrugged. What Mark was suggesting went against every fiber of his being. He wanted to fight this divorce business, not stand back and allow it to happen. He was an activist at heart, not a passive bystander. "I don't know, Mark."

"Well, think about it. I know you'll do what's right." Mark stood and headed for the door. "Sure you don't want to come to Barb and Glen's for awhile? There'll probably be some homemade pizza later and Barb is a great cook."

Brent shook his head. "I don't think I'd be good company tonight. But thanks."

Mark shrugged into his leather jacket. "What about tomorrow morning? You still coming to church?"

Brent nodded.

"Good. Bible study is first at 9:30. The worship service follows at 10:45."

"I'll be there," Brent promised, seeing his friend out.

Then he strode back into the living room. He thought about phoning Kori, but decided to let her cool off until at least tomorrow. Was she with that fiancé of hers tonight? Brent heaved a curt laugh as he sat back down in the chair. Nothing like pushing her into the other man's arms by threatening her. Of course she'd run to Jared after what he'd said to her tonight. What could he have been thinking?

Brent sat there pensively for many long minutes. Finally, he decided on a hot shower. Then he'd spend the evening reading. He'd brought an entire box of books from California in hopes of catching up on the reading he had never seemed to find time for in the past. But he had the time now. He had two and a half months of time.

But will that be long enough, he mused, *to win back Kori's heart?*

&

"Where'd you get these roses, girlfriend?" Susie, another medical assistant, asked Kori the following Monday morning. Lifting the box and putting her nose into the flowers, the young, African-American woman, inhaled deeply. "They smell as pretty as they look."

Kori smiled, nodding. "Roses are my favorite. And these are quite a surprise. Of course, they're from Jared. He's been deer hunting all weekend. Maybe he missed me."

"I guess," Susie replied taking another whiff. "And he must have missed you bad, too, because roses aren't exactly cheap these days."

A warm feeling flooded Kori's insides. So Jared was a bit of a romantic after all. Then she opened the card which had come with the roses. It read:

Dearest Kori,
  Please accept my sincere apologies for the senseless remarks I made Saturday night. The last thing I want to do is fight with you. I love you.

Brent

"That man is out of his very mind!" Kori declared, crumpling the card and tossing it into the wastebasket.

"Who, Jared?" Susie stood up, her black braids swinging. The colorful beads in her hair clicked as they collided and she frowned at Kori's dismay. "What are you talking about?"

Kori shook her head. "Never mind. It's. . .it's a misunderstanding."

"What's a misunderstanding?" Ryan asked, appearing at the doorway of the medical assistants' station. He smiled when he saw the flowers. "Are those yours, Kori?" he asked with a wry grin.

"Sure are," said Susie, "but I don't think they're from Jared."

Kori gave Susie a pointed stare while Ryan's brows shot up in surprise. Then he chuckled.

Kori, meanwhile, gathered the box of flowers from her desktop and headed down the hallway.

"Hey, where are you taking those?" Susie called after her.

"I'm going to put them at the front desk," Kori replied, turning on her heel. "I think the receptionists could use some roses on a Monday morning."

"You got that right," Susie muttered.

With a nod, Kori resumed her mission. Mondays were this staff's worst days. On Mondays it seemed like half the clinic's growing population took ill and then called, demanding appointments. And, because they were feeling sick, they accepted no excuses. The poor receptionists became verbal punching bags if a doctor's schedule was full.

"Look what I brought you guys," Kori said, setting the roses in front of Vicki, a red-haired receptionist.

"For us?" she asked, her green eyes shining.

"For you. You can split them between you and Gigi."

"And where, may I ask, did these come from?" Vicki teased with batting lashes. "Or should I say, *who* did these come from?"

Kori felt a slight blush warming her cheeks. Vicki had been the one to call up and announce that a florist had just delivered a box of roses.

"Don't ask. Just enjoy. Okay?"

"Okay," Vicki said, giving Gigi a curious look.

Gigi put two phone calls on hold. "Did you and Jared have a falling-out?"

Kori shook her head. All her friends at work knew Jared. He came into the clinic at least once a week to "check on his best girl."

Kori grinned. "Look, you guys, I said *don't ask.* Just take the flowers and have a good Monday."

Both women groaned as the telephone rang again.

Smiling Kori turned and went back upstairs. Ryan met her in front of the exam rooms.

"What does our schedule look like today?"

"Booked and double-booked. We'll be here until seven tonight."

Ryan grimaced. "There's a missions' conference at church. I was hoping to make tonight's service."

"Well, if you don't chitchat with the patients," Kori advised with a teasing smile, "you might make it."

Ryan lifted a brow. "Are you insinuating that I take too much time with my patients?"

"Not insinuating, Ryan. I'm telling you. Again."

He laughed, a warm, rich sound that never failed to make Kori smile.

"Do we have any patients waiting right now?"

Kori shook her head. "Our first patient isn't due until nine o'clock—forty minutes from now."

"Good. I'd like to talk to you. Let's go into my office."

Kori nodded and followed Ryan. "You're not going to insist that I come to your church again, are you?" she asked, taking the chair in front of his desk. A matching credenza and bookshelf lined the wall directly behind Ryan.

He shook his head. "No, I won't insist. But you're always welcome. You know that. But what I want to tell you sort of has to do with my church." Ryan folded his hands and, with elbows on his desk, he rested his chin on his knuckles. "I met your husband yesterday. . .at church."

"Oh, good grief," Kori said, sitting back in the chair.

"He's a friend of Mark Henley whose fiancée Julia is one of Stacie's friends. When we were introduced, I made the comment that my medical assistant's last name is McDonald also, after which Brent asked, 'Her first name wouldn't be Kori, would it?' " Ryan chuckled. "Small world."

"Extremely," Kori replied facetiously.

"Then we had dinner together, Brent, Mark, Julia, Stacie, and me."

"Lovely."

Ryan was grinning at her sarcasm. "And, judging from your response to the roses, I take it he's the one who sent them."

Kori nodded, considering Ryan through a narrowed gaze. "How much did Brent tell you?"

"Hardly anything. . .just that he *isn't* your ex-husband."

The fight and sarcasm went out of Kori as the unbelievable truth once more hit her heart. She was still married—married to Brent!

"I haven't had a chance to tell Jared yet," Kori uttered before Ryan could ask.

"Any chance of reconciliation between you and Brent?"

Kori shook her head. "None."

"Hmm. . ."

"Listen, Ryan, I know Brent. He changes like the wind, blowing one direction and then another. He only wants to reconcile with me because. . .well, I figure it's because Mark reconciled with his high school sweetheart and now he and Julia are going to be married. Brent is one of the groomsmen."

Ryan nodded. "Yes, I heard that yesterday, too."

"So Brent probably got it in his head that he wants what Mark has—a resurrected love affair."

Ryan shrugged. "I guess you'd know."

Kori thought the comment had a dismissive ring to it, so she rose from the chair. "I'll go see if our first patient has arrived. Maybe we can get a jump start on the day." She turned, but at the office door, she paused. "Ryan, is this going to affect our working relationship?"

He sat back in his chair, considering her. "I don't know what you mean."

"Well, you're a Christian and so is Brent, you're a doctor and so is Brent. I'm sure you guys will soon be fast friends, and you'll take his side over mine. . .if you haven't already."

"I haven't taken anyone's *side,* Kori, and I don't expect to. But I will say that it would thrill my heart to see your marriage restored."

"Ryan, two years ago Brent said he didn't love me anymore. Don't you remember how much that hurt me?"

"Yes, you and I have had many heart-to-heart talks about how hurt you were. You know I understand, Kori."

She nodded, putting her hands on her hips. "So now after my broken heart is finally beginning to heal and I'm getting my life back together, I'm supposed to forget the devastation Brent imposed upon me and slip back into the role of his wife?" She shook her head. "I don't think so."

"It's called forgiveness, Kori."

She shook her head once more. "It's called not being stupid twice." With that, she left Ryan's office and called for their first patient, Keith Baxter.

While Ryan was in with Mr. Baxter, Kori brought their second patient into an exam room. Sara Rondel, a mother of two, had another cold and possibly strep throat. Kori logged her patient's temperature and blood pressure in the chart before hanging it on the outside of the door as she left the exam room.

As Ryan's assistant, Kori could do as much as he allowed, and Kori did everything, it seemed, except give intravenous fluids, otherwise known as IVs. Those were the responsibility of the clinic's "triage nurse" who was a licensed RN.

On to patient number three.

Little Joey Thompson was here for his six-month checkup. Since Ryan was a family practice physician, many of his patients were children. In the exam room, Kori had Mrs. Thompson undress her baby. Then Kori weighed him and logged Mrs. Thompson's remarks and concerns in Joey's chart. Everything was fine; the child seemed to be very healthy. But he'd need an immunization shot today—he'd missed his last one because of an ear infection.

"I always feel so mean when I do this," Kori told Mrs. Thompson, who held Joey on her lap. Ryan had already examined the boy. "I try to remember," she said as the needle penetrated the fat of Joey's thigh, "that inoculations save children's lives. I'm actually doing them a favor when I give them a shot."

Joey screamed at the injection, but Kori was fast and efficient and soon Mrs. Thompson was soothing away her baby's tears. Then, after advising the mother what to do in the case of fever and soreness in the baby's leg, Kori went on to the next patient. However, she was now behind, having spent so much time with the Thompsons.

Three patients were waiting and one of them was Mrs. Trumble, an elderly patient who could talk up a lather. Kori sighed.

By the end of the day, she was exhausted. Ryan left at 6:30, giving Kori instructions to call back several patients with advice. She also had some prescriptions to call into pharmacies and there were, of course, all her route slips to complete for billing purposes. In addition, Kori had to get tomorrow's charts in order—and all before she could leave for her eight o'clock appointment with Tamara Mills, the attorney who was a friend of Clair's.

Roses or no roses, Kori was still filing for divorce.

&

"It's going to cost me. . .how much?" Kori stared in disbelief at the solemn-faced attorney before her.

Sitting behind her wide, impressive desk, Tamara Mills was a stoic professional, a no-nonsense lawyer, and Kori was convinced that she was every bit as good as Clair had said; however, this woman's fees were atrocious!

"Here's the invoice," Tamara said. "It's itemized. There's a retaining fee and filing fees."

The figures swam before Kori's eyes. This divorce business was going to cost her a thousand dollars. . .up front. Paying for it would break her savings account.

"How long do you think it will take—the whole divorce process, I mean?" Kori pulled out her checkbook.

"Divorces take about a year."

"A year?"

Tamara gave her a patient smile. "Yes. Court dates take a while to obtain." She cleared her throat. "And please be aware that the process could take longer, if your estranged spouse decides to put up a fight."

Kori grimaced. She was certain that she had the fight of her life ahead of her.

"Now then," Tamara said, "do you know your husband's address here in Milwaukee?"

Kori shook her head.

"Well, no matter." Tamara grinned. "We'll find him." Standing, the woman clad in a stylish skirt, matching jacket, and white silk blouse, extended her hand to Kori. "A pleasure doing business with you. I'll be in touch."

Kori nodded, shaking the other woman's hand. Then she gave her the check.

As she left the attorney's office, Kori remembered that her car hadn't been running well lately. She only hoped that it wasn't anything serious since she wasn't going to have extra money for awhile. She didn't make a whole lot at the clinic. Twelve dollars an hour. She paid three hundred dollars a month in rent, as did Clair and Dana, and she had her share of the bills to pay.

Kori breathed a sigh of relief when her car started right up. She breathed another as she pulled into the parking lot of her apartment complex. "Just be a good car," she told it, "and don't break down on me for a least a month, okay?"

Then, climbing out of her Chevette into the frosty November night, Kori resented the fact that she was even in this position. Brent should pay for some of this, shouldn't he? He was the one who left her initially with threats of divorce. It wasn't her fault that Tom Sandersfeld hadn't filed the official papers.

But it was my fault for not following up, Kori admitted to herself.

Earlier this year when she had filed her taxes, the IRS sent her a letter stating the reasons she couldn't file a single return. She had meant to contact Brent about it—but it was just after his father died, and Kori hadn't wanted to add what she thought were mere technicalities to his grief. So she corrected her tax return, collected her refund, and put off contacting Brent until she had all but forgotten about it. Until now. Until he showed up and announced that they were still married.

But this will never happen again, she vowed. *I will never be so irresponsible in any relationship again. Never!*

This, however, brought Kori to another realization. She had to tell Jared, and she'd have to tell him soon. Tonight, in fact. She would tell him tonight!

six

Kori drove down Cleveland Avenue, grateful to have borrowed Clair's car tonight. "Hey, what are big sisters for?" she'd said, tossing Kori the keys. Kori, on the other hand, was certain she'd developed paranoia now solely because she had exhausted her savings on Tamara Mills' fees. But logic dictated that she couldn't control whether her car broke down or where it broke down. She'd just have to deal with the problem if or when it occurred.

Reaching her fiancé's house, Kori gulped down her nervousness as she pulled alongside the curb and parked the car. Jared owned his own home, a three bedroom bungalow on Milwaukee's southwest side. The neighborhood was occupied by primarily blue-collar workers, like Jared, and kept up with hardworking pride.

Kori climbed the front porch stairs and then rang the doorbell. The window on the wooden door was too high for her to see inside, but the house was well-lit. Jared had to be home.

"Kori!" he said with surprise, opening the door. "What are you doing here?" She heard male voices whooping and hollering from inside the house. He grinned. "Monday Night Football."

"Oh, I forgot."

He laughed. "Never mind. Come on in."

Following Jared into the house, Kori took off her coat and hung it on hooks fastened to the wall in the tiny foyer. Then she entered the living room where blue clouds of cigar smoke hung in the air. Beer and soda cans littered the coffee table along with a box of Ritz crackers and an empty plate.

"Hi, you guys," she said to the five men perched on the couch, love seat, and miscellaneous kitchen chairs.

Her salutation was met with hearty words of welcome as Jared plopped back into his recliner.

"Would you mind filling up that plate, honey, with the cheese and sausage in the fridge?"

Kori smiled at the request. "No, I don't mind at all." And she didn't either.

Fetching the plate off the coffee table, Kori walked from the living room, though the dining room, passing Jared's pool table. She hoped to one day restore his billiard area into a formal dining room, and she could well imagine the dinner parties here with friends while their children slept soundly in the bedrooms upstairs. . .

Kori entered the kitchen where various small engine parts lined the counters. *Too bad Jared doesn't know how to fix car engines,* she mused, taking the venison sausage from the refrigerator. Slicing it, she thought about how nicely some blue-and-white country curtains would look on the bare kitchen windows. Why Jared wasn't bothered that his neighbors could see right into his kitchen, especially at night, escaped Kori. She liked pulled shades and closed draperies at night. She thought it was warm and cozy. Even more, she liked to open them up in the morning like a surprise present and see how the day had dawned. But Jared said he didn't care one way or the other.

Would he mind if I wanted new linoleum? she wondered after accidentally dropping a piece of sausage skin. *I'll bet Jared hasn't given this ugly floor a good scrubbing in all the years he's lived here.*

After arranging the sausage on the plate, Kori began slicing the cheddar cheese. She thought back to a couple of months ago when Jared had asked her to move in with him. Kori refused the offer, saying she wasn't living with any man who wasn't her husband. The same held true for giving her body to a man—Kori maintained she'd have to be married to him first. She wasn't pious. She had just been raised a conservative country girl whose parents instilled in her a high moral standard. So then Jared proposed marriage. Kori accepted. And, though she hadn't given herself to Jared physically, she had mentally. Now, if only he could win her heart. . .

"Aw, Kori, you don't have to do anything fancy with that," he said, entering the kitchen. "The guys are just going to shove that cheese and sausage into their mouths. They don't care if it looks nice on the plate." Laughing, Jared took the "hors d'oeuvres" and gave Kori such an exuberant kiss on her cheek that he nearly knocked her backward.

"Jared, I need to talk to you," she called to his retreating back.

"Okay, it's almost halftime," he replied over his shoulder.

With a sigh, Kori opened the refrigerator and pulled out a diet cola. Leaning against the sink, since all the kitchen chairs were in the living room, she sipped her drink and listened to "the guys" carrying on. *My word,* she thought, *but they're noisy. And funny.* Kori smiled at some of the ridiculous jokes that drifted to her ears.

"So what's on your mind?" Jared asked, when halftime came some ten minutes later. "You've got twenty minutes to tell me." He smiled, adding, "You sure are pretty."

Arms around her waist, he closed in on her for a kiss but Kori pushed him back. She suddenly envisioned Brent's face in her mind's eye, then heard his voice, saying, "We're still married, Kori." She almost felt his presence there, and was repulsed by her situation.

"Oh, Jared," she fairly croaked.

He brought back his chin in surprise. "What's wrong?"

"Something horrible happened this weekend."

"What?" He actually looked alarmed now as a deep frown furrowed his sand-colored brows.

Kori swallowed. "Well. . .it's my ex-husband, Brent."

"Yeah, what about him?"

She swallowed again. "Well. . ."

"Well, what?"

"Shhh, Jared, please keep your voice down."

"Well, then, spit it out, honey," he said impatiently. "The

guys are waiting for me."

Kori nodded. "Okay. Brent is in town and he contacted me because. . .well. . .well, something accidentally went wrong with our divorce papers and now we have to get divorced all over again."

Jared narrowed his gaze. "What do you mean?"

"I mean, I had to get a lawyer. I saw her tonight, and I've got to file for divorce because. . .well, because. . ."

"Kori, just say it, will you?"

"I'm still married!"

Jared gaped at her, his rugged features a mixture of incredulity and fury.

Kori lowered her gaze. "I'm sorry, Jared."

"Why?"

She looked back at him, puzzled. "Why, what? Why am I sorry? Or why am I still married?"

"Both!" Jared shook his head. "Oh, never mind."

"Jared, I'm going to fix it," Kori promised. "I've hired a lawyer, and—"

"What about our cruise in February?"

Kori tried not to grimace. She knew he'd be disappointed at the news. "It'll have to wait. You see, that's what I'm sorry about." She sighed, weary as much from this divorce business as she was from her busy day at the clinic. "It's going to take about a year."

"A year! Did you hear what you just said? A whole year!?"

Kori's heart suddenly pounded with fear. "If you love me, you'll wait," she said hopefully. "If you love me, you'll stand by me and—"

"Listen, Kori, go ask Dave out there about his divorce," he said, nodding toward the living room. "It was a nightmare. And then, after all was said and done—or so he thought—Dave's ex-wife sued his girlfriend for something really stupid."

"Oh, Brent would never sue you, if that's what you're worried about."

"Can you get that in writing?"

Kori bit her lip. *Not likely,* she thought.

Jared shook his head. "One of the reasons I got involved with you, Kori," he said soberly, "was because your divorce was far enough behind you so as it wouldn't affect me." He waved his arm. "You think I want to lose my house?"

She looked at him, her heart ready to break. "Is your house more important than me?"

"Yes! I mean, no! I mean. . ." Jared threw his hands in the air. "I don't know!"

Kori willed herself not to cry as Jared circled the kitchen irritably. She had been hoping for a more gallant response to this. She had been hoping to hear Jared say he loved her and he'd wait a hundred years to marry her if he had to!

However, Kori was beginning to understand that real love was nothing like the love in fairy tales and romance novels— or, then again, maybe men today weren't anything like fictional heros.

"I need some time to think about this," Jared muttered.

Kori nodded. Then she watched as he pulled a beer from the refrigerator and left the kitchen for his friends and the football game.

❧

Two days later, Brent hailed her in the parking lot of the clinic. The day was sunny, but the wind had a bite to it—and so did Kori.

"What do you want?"

Brent looked a bit taken aback by her vehemence. "I just wanted to. . ." He looked at his watch. "Are you late?"

"Yep." She pushed past him.

"Kori, wait. Please. I'd like to talk to you. I've been trying to phone you. I've left messages. . ."

She whirled on him. "Look, Brent, I don't want to talk to you. Can't you get that through your head? You are ruining my life for a second time! All I want for you to do is go away—or drop dead, whichever is more convenient."

Brent grinned wryly. "Well, I'm glad you haven't lost your

sense of humor."

Kori glared at him. Then she turned and continued walking.

"Hey, did you like the roses I sent on Monday?"

She stopped in midstride. *I will not let him bait me.*

Brent was directly behind her now. He touched the shoulder of her full-length, grey wool coat. "You could just say. . . thanks. That's simple enough. Or you could say that you accept my apology for the harsh way I spoke to you last Saturday night. I'd like to hear that—that you forgive me. Or you could say you liked the roses. I know they're your favorite flowers."

Slowly, Kori turned to face him, her cheeks flaming with anger despite the frigid temperatures. "Brent, my lawyer said you'll receive divorce papers in about a week. All I'm going to say to you this morning is. . .*sign them!*"

With that, she resumed her walk to the front door of the medical clinic, leaving Brent, literally, out in the cold.

≈

Brent hung up the telephone after talking to Attorney Tamara Mills's legal assistant. She had wanted his address. He said he wouldn't give it to her. He said he was going to be very uncooperative and that Kori's attorney should consider herself fairly warned.

"We'll get your address anyway," the legal assistant replied. "I've got your phone number and we'll be able to track you down. Just thought I might save myself—and our client— some time and money."

"Guess again," Brent retorted. Then he'd hung up.

Walking through the living room now, he remembered what Kori told him yesterday. *You are ruining my life for a second time!* It pained him again to realize that he'd ruined her life even once.

Lord, I don't want to hurt her anymore, he prayed. *I just want a second chance. Am I really asking too much?*

No, he wasn't asking too much of God. He knew that. With God, nothing was impossible. But maybe. . .maybe he was asking too much of Kori.

Lord, I'm not good at waiting and I don't want to cooperate with Kori's attorney. But she's so angry with me. . .Kori won't even talk to me. How can I get her to reconcile when she can hardly bear the sight of me?

And then that still small voice seemed to reply, "Love her, Brent. Just love her."

Maybe I'm not good at that, either.

It occurred to Brent, then, that he'd have to learn to be good at it. And he'd have to rely on God to help him. Picking up his Bible from the coffee table, he opened it to the page he'd marked months ago. 1 Corinthians 13: *Love is patient, love is kind. It does not envy, it does not boast, it is not proud. It is not rude, it is not self-seeking, it is not easily angered, it keeps no record of wrongs. Love does not delight in evil but rejoices with the truth. It always protects, always trusts, always hopes, always perseveres. Love never fails.*

Releasing a long, slow whistle, Brent thought the same thing he did every time he read that passage: It was one tall order!

All right, Lord, I'll cooperate—except it goes against everything in me. And I'll not speak harshly to Kori or threaten her any more. Brent sighed, picking up the telephone book, looking for Tamara Mills's number. *But I ask You, Lord, to intervene and stop this divorce.*

"Well, Mr. McDonald, what a surprise," the legal assistant said once she came to the phone. "I didn't expect to hear from you again. Are you calling so you can be more uncooperative?" She laughed.

"It's Dr. McDonald," he replied with all the politeness he could muster through a clenched jaw. He hated to do this—to give in. He'd rather fight; however, it seemed this battle was the Lord's.

He gave the legal assistant his address and she repeated it back to him.

"Yes, that's correct. Oh, and one more thing. . .I'd like you to document something." Brent paused in momentary thought. "I'd like you to note that I love my wife and I don't want a divorce. I've changed my mind about cooperating, but only because I don't want to hurt Kori."

"Dr. McDonald," the legal assistant began, "that's something *your* attorney should document. Not us. Good-bye."

Brent looked at the phone and then slammed down the receiver. He should have known *they* wouldn't cooperate!

With a sigh, Brent looked at his wristwatch. 6:15. Apparently Attorney Mills had evening hours.

Picking up the phone again, Brent dialed Kori's number. She wasn't home before and Brent had to force himself not to ask if she was out with Jared. He couldn't stand the thought of Kori and that guy together, yet he couldn't stand the not-knowing either. So he prayed, asking God to somehow break up that relationship so he could move in and win back his wife's heart.

"Kori's not home," Clair said once more. "She must be running late at the clinic again. Can I take a message?"

"If I leave one, will you promise to give it to her?"

"I promise." Clair paused. "Listen, Brent, just for the record, I'm not taking sides here."

Brent smiled wryly. "I appreciate it."

"So, what's the message?"

"Tell Kori that. . .well, tell her I'm cooperating with her attorney but only because. . .because I love her and I don't want to hurt her further. Okay?"

Clair was silent for a full minute and Brent didn't know if she was writing his message down or just thinking it over.

Finally, she said, "You know, that's really sweet, Brent. I'll tell her."

seven

Kori unlocked the apartment door, realizing that it had only been one week since Brent's first phone call. One week and now her life was falling apart just like her car.

"You look bushed," Dana stated, as Kori hung up her coat and walked into the living room. "Tough day?"

"Not really. I'm just stressed out."

Clair called a "hello" from the kitchen, adding, "How come you're so late?"

"My car wouldn't start," Kori replied, collapsing into the armchair. "I'm just lucky I was in the clinic's parking lot at the time. The unfortunate part is that I had to call a tow truck, which costs more money than the car is practically worth. But the driver was nice enough to drop me off here at home before taking my car to the shop." She sighed. "I guess I really shouldn't be surprised, either. I knew this was coming by the way it's been acting lately."

"I hope it's nothing serious," Clair said, coming into the room. "And you know I'll share my car with you when I can."

Kori managed a tired smile. "Thanks, sis."

"Hey, have you got plans tonight?"

Kori shook her head, feeling even more miserable. "Jared went deer hunting. He'll be gone for the next week." What she didn't say was he never called to tell her good-bye. *He's still angry,* she thought fretfully. *What if he breaks our engagement?*

"Earth to Kori," Clair called to her. "Come in, Kori."

She shook off her musings. "Sorry about that. What were you saying?"

Clair left the kitchen and stood before her. "I said. . .Brent called about an hour ago. He wants you to call him back."

"Forget it."

The telephone rang and Dana jumped for the cordless phone. "Oh, hi, Brent," she said as Kori rolled her eyes in aggravation. "Yeah, she's here now. Her car broke down. Here, I'll put her on." Dana held out the phone. "For you."

"I'm not here."

"Oh, yes, you are. I see you with my own two eyes."

"A hallucination."

Dana frowned. "I do not hallucinate!"

"Oh, give me that telephone," Clair said, leaving the kitchen and giving Kori one of her long, preprimand looks.

"Brent," she explained, "Kori is playing hard to get and she won't talk to you. Sorry." Clair paused, listening to his reply. Then she covered the phone, looking back at Kori. "He wants to come over and cook dinner for you. . .for all of us."

"Oh, say yes, Kori," Dana pleaded. "Zach is out of town till Sunday and Tim is working late so Clair and I don't have anything to do tonight."

"And you want Brent to cook for us?" Throwing her head back, Kori hooted. "He can't even boil water!"

"Hear that, Brent? She's laughing at your offer." Clair paused, smiling and listening to the response. "Okay, I'll tell her." She covered the phone again. "He says he took some cooking classes and now he's like the Galloping Gourmet, or something."

"Oh, right," Kori said facetiously. "Knowing Brent, it means he learned to turn on the oven and throw in a frozen pizza."

"Did you hear her, Brent? She doesn't believe you." Clair paused momentarily before turning back to Kori. "Brent wants to know if your favorite food is still Italian?"

"Yes, it is, but—"

"She says yes, Brent. Okay, I'll relay the message." With that, Clair clicked off the phone.

Kori lifted a brow expectantly.

"He's on his way over."

"What?" Kori stood up, glaring at her sister.

"I'm hungry, okay? And Brent is offering to cook up an Italian feast!"

Dana was grinning from ear to ear. "Oh, good, I'm hungry too. Besides, I'm curious to see if Brent's a better cook than I am."

Kori groaned. "Look, you guys, I don't want Brent to come over tonight. I've spent my savings on filing for a divorce. I want him out of my life!"

Clair held out the telephone to her. "Fine. Then you call Brent and tell him that." She narrowed her gaze in serious speculation. "You're going to have to talk to him some time, Kori, be it tonight, tomorrow, or the next day. You can't just wish the man away."

"I know," Kori replied solemnly, "I tried it already."

Clair laughed.

"Hey, I've got it, Kori. Why not try being Brent's friend?" Dana suggested with a smile. "I know a woman at work who's divorced and she and her ex-husband are friends. In fact, she had some fund-raiser to attend at the Performing Arts Center and she couldn't get a date, so she asked her ex and he escorted her." Dana tipped her pretty blond head. "Now why can't you and Brent be friends like that?"

"Yeah, Kori," Clair said. "You know, a person can never have enough friends and Brent is trying to be so nice. . ."

Kori rolled her eyes. Brent was a charmer, all right.

"And if you and Brent were friends," Clair continued, "you wouldn't be so stressed out. You two could settle this divorce stuff much more effectively and without lasting emotional scars."

"That's right, Kori. My aunt's divorce took years just because she and her ex kept fighting over the settlements."

"It took *years?*" Kori certainly didn't want that. One year was long enough! She quickly weighed her options. If she and Brent were "friends," she might have an easier time of things, just like Clair said, and there was no real reason *not* to be his friend. Brent had already stated that he'd cooperate. He wasn't fighting her or the divorce proceedings anymore. Maybe he'd even agree to pay half of her attorney fees so she could get her car fixed.

And if they were "friends," Brent might agree to assure Jared, in writing, that he wasn't going to sue him. Then Jared might not be tempted to break off their engagement.

"Maybe you guys are right," Kori finally conceded. "Maybe Brent and I could just be friends."

"You could at least give it a try," Clair replied. "What have you got to lose?"

Certainly not my heart, Kori thought with a shrugged reply to her sister's question. Then she walked into her bedroom to change clothes, thinking, *I want Jared to have my heart so Brent will never be able to break it again!*

❧

Brent whistled happily as he drove to Kori's apartment. He felt like the luckiest man in the world. Kori had agreed, albeit reluctantly, to let him come over and cook for her.

Thank You, Lord, he whispered prayerfully as he reached her apartment complex.

Parking his truck, Brent grabbed the two bags of groceries he had purchased on the way over. A one-pound box of pasta, cans of tomato paste, sauce, a can of crushed tomatoes, ground beef, a garlic bulb, oregano, an onion, and fresh mushrooms. Brent was prepared to make Kori and her roommates the best mostoccoli they had ever tasted. He'd also bought a fresh loaf of Italian bread, a head of lettuce, and, of course, Italian salad dressing.

Brent suddenly chuckled, remembering Kori's reaction to his cooking. He couldn't blame her one bit for laughing. It was true; he hadn't been able to even boil water a few years ago. But in order to survive as a bachelor, Brent decided he'd have to learn a few things on his own, like doing laundry and cooking. And the latter he'd had to learn by taking evening classes at a local high school.

So now he'd show her. He'd prove to Kori that he wasn't at all the helpless, demanding, self-centered man who had left her two and a half years ago. Why, he could even iron a shirt without scorching it now!

Brent let himself into the small foyer of the apartment building. Rows of mailboxes lined one wall while a row of buzzers were on the other. Ringing Kori's apartment, he waited only a few minutes before Kori herself came down to let him in.

"You could have just buzzed me up," he said, entering the warm, homey-looking lobby. "You could have saved yourself a trip."

Kori shrugged and Brent thought she looked tired. "I wanted to talk to you before. . .well, I didn't want Clair or Dana to overhear our conversation." She looked at the bags in his hands. "Want some help?"

Brent nodded gratefully and handed her the lighter of the two. Then they walked toward the elevator.

"So what did you want to talk to me about?"

Kori waited a moment until the elevator door opened and they walked into the car. She pushed the button for the second floor. "Brent, I know you said you want to resume a marital relationship with me, but quite honestly, I'm not interested. I haven't been your wife for over two years and it's a role I don't want. Like I said before, it took me a long time to get over you but now I. . .I am!" But something in her voice made Brent doubt it. "And I'm going to marry Jared!"

Brent guarded himself against a defensive reply. He knew what Kori said was an honest response as well as a deserving consequence for him, and yet he just couldn't accept them. He simply was not a man to give up that easily.

"So what I propose," Kori continued, causing him to tune back in, "is that we commit ourselves to developing a friendship—a platonic friendship."

"A *friendship?*" Brent furrowed his brows, somewhat surprised.

Kori looked him right in the eye and nodded. "A *platonic* friendship," she emphasized once more. "Do you think it's possible, Brent? I mean, wouldn't it be better for both of us if we came to some sort of truce?"

"I don't know. . ."

The elevator opened. They both stepped out onto the floor and headed for Kori's apartment. She stopped, however, a few feet away from the door.

"So what do you say, Brent? Are we friends. . .or enemies? There is no in-between for us."

Looking down into her tired face and sad-looking eyes, Brent didn't think he could really be Kori's enemy. Not anymore. He really did love her.

Then he recalled Mark's suggestion. *Why don't you try being her friend for awhile, Brent? Then you can ask for a second chance at the husband role.*

Brent smiled, his decision made. "Kori, I would feel honored to be your friend," he said gallantly as his smile broadened. "Friends it is. Want to shake on it?" He shifted the grocery bag, then held out his right hand.

Kori narrowed her eyes suspiciously. "You're giving in awfully easily, Brent. That's not like you. I thought I'd have to at least threaten you."

He laughed, shrugging his shoulders beneath his navy-blue down ski jacket. "Yeah, well, you didn't think I could cook, either, but I can. You'll see. I hope you're hungry."

For the first time tonight, Brent saw Kori smile as she slipped her hand into his. "Friends!" she declared. "And, yes, I'm starving, so you'd better get busy."

With that, Kori let him into the apartment.

eight

Kori watched Brent create his spaghetti sauce while Clair and Dana set the table. "You know," she said at last, "if I hadn't seen it, I would have never believed it."

He grinned wryly. "And I'm not even finished yet."

"Smells great!" Dana declared, coming back into the kitchen area.

From where she sat on a tall stool beside the stove, Kori agreed. She wanted to watch Brent's every move, and she was amazed at what she was seeing. He had deftly crushed the garlic, chopped the fresh mushrooms, browned the ground beef, and added the tomatoes and spices—all by himself. A real feat for the Brent McDonald she used to know.

"So, you took some classes. . .?"

Brent nodded, stirring the sauce that was nearly boiling. "I got sick of fast food and the hospital's cafeteria food, so I figured I'd better learn to cook."

"Oh, come on, Brent," Clair said, sitting down on a stool beside Kori. A teasing gleam entered her eyes. "You could have just found some nurses to cook for you. On the TV show I watch, those ER doctors are never without women."

Brent laughed. "Clair, a real-life emergency room isn't anything like Hollywood's. Between my patients and all the paperwork, I don't have time to act like the doctors do on television—not that I would anyway. And I'll admit that occasionally romances spring up between doctors and nurses, but what you see on television, Clair, would be considered scandalous and grossly unprofessional if it happened in real life, at least it would in the hospitals I'm affiliated with."

"Well, thanks for setting me straight, Brent," Clair said with a little chuckle. "But I was only kidding."

He shrugged and turned the burner on a lower setting since his spaghetti sauce had come to a full boil. "I might as well confess that I said all that more for Kori's benefit than yours, Clair." He smiled, looking more amused than contrite.

"Oh, I get it," Dana interjected. "You don't want Kori getting funny ideas about ER docs, huh?"

"Exactly," Brent replied, giving Kori a meaningful glance.

She just turned away. "I'll get the plates out," she announced, changing the subject. Walking over to the cupboard, Kori pulled down four plates from the shelf. *I thought we agreed to be friends,* she fumed, *and friends don't give each other the kind of looks Brent just gave me.*

"Actually," Brent added, "I don't want *any* of you ladies to get funny ideas about ER docs."

Curiosity won over anger, and Kori turned back around.

"I just want to be a friend to Kori—to all of you," Brent said, defusing Kori altogether, "so I want you to know exactly where I'm coming from."

"So, doctors aren't really like they are on TV, huh?" Dana asked with a hint of disappointment. "They seem so macho and cool and like. . .they know *everything!* You'd just have to trust them with your life."

Brent chuckled. "To tell you the truth, I don't watch a lot of television."

Clair smacked her palm against her forehead and Kori laughed. Brent was laughing, too, although poor Dana just stood there looking totally confused.

"Dana," Clair said, putting a hand on her shoulder, "Brent is being a wise guy."

"Oh. . .so you really *are* like the doctors on TV."

Brent shook his head.

"Dana," Clair said, giving her a mild shake this time, "Brent's not like the doctors on that nighttime drama you watch every week, only it's funny because he's never seen the show."

"I've heard enough about it to make a judgment call, though," he said in his own defense.

"Oh, I get it," Dana said, rolling her eyes, and everyone laughed all over again.

By the time the sauce had sufficiently simmered, the pasta cooked, and dinner was served, Kori was feeling much more at ease around Brent. As they ate, they talked about movies, hobbies, and jobs—all very safe topics—and Kori thought it was a pleasant and most tasty dinner. The wall of hostility she'd set up between them seemed to be crumbling.

"I'm impressed, Brent," Kori admitted, clearing the dining room table afterward. "That was one of the best Italian dinners I've eaten in a long while."

"Thank you," he replied with a little bow and a broad smile.

"Could have used a little more oregano," Dana remarked over her shoulder on the way to the kitchen area.

"Ah, the critic speaks," Clair said with a chuckle. "Don't worry, Brent, Dana doesn't think anyone cooks as well as she does."

Brent was still smiling. "You like to cook, too?"

Dana nodded. "Except I didn't start cooking out of necessity like you did. For me, cooking is therapeutic."

"And she needs a lot of therapy," Clair teased, "so she's cooking all the time."

"Oh, quiet," Dana retorted.

"Now, girls, behave yourselves," Kori facetiously admonished them. "Remember, we have company."

"Yes, Mother," both Clair and Dana said in unison. Then they all laughed.

"Oh, don't look so confused, Brent," Dana told him, smiling. "Every once in a while, Kori has to practice her mom bit for after she and Jared get married and have kids. Isn't that right, Kori?"

"Right," she replied, trying to sound determined. However, some of that old uneasiness was creeping back into her heart. Jared wasn't happy about her situation and the very point of contention was standing three feet away.

With her arms full of dishes, Kori walked into the kitchen

and began filling the sink.

"Let those dishes go," Clair said. "Let's put on a movie and relax before we wash them."

Kori shook her head. "You guys go ahead. I'll clean up here." She paused before adding, "I don't really feel like watching a movie anyway."

Clair shrugged. "Suit yourself." Turning, she asked Brent, "Are you coming?"

"No, I'll wash and Kori can dry. I don't feel like watching a movie either."

"Okay, then Dana and I will start the movie without you two."

Clair crossed the living room to where Dana was already sorting through the collection of classic videos.

Kori turned around and set the dishes into the sink filled with soapy water. "You don't have to help me, Brent. There's not much here."

"I insist," he said, pushing up the sleeves of his shirt. It was a brown cotton knit shirt with a collar, and it matched nicely with Brent's brown, casual pants. But Kori wasn't surprised; Brent had always been fashion-minded and coordinated to a fault.

He dipped his hands into the water and Kori picked up a dish towel. Standing beside him now, she got a whiff of his cologne. It was the same sweet, manly scent that he always wore, and Kori had to fight back an onslaught of memories. Good memories. Memories of being crazy in love with Brent McDonald.

Don't think about the past, Kori told herself, drying a plate and putting it away in the cupboard. *This is the present and Brent and I are just friends.*

"So your car broke down, huh?" Brent asked.

Kori nodded, but then suddenly remembered her plan.

"You, know, Brent, I'm in kind of a bind," she hedged. "I had to pay my attorney a lot of money toward our divorce proceedings, and now I don't have enough funds to repair my car. So. . .I was wondering. . .well, since we're friends now, and since you're not contesting the divorce—"

"I'll help you, Kori," Brent replied easily.

She was surprised. That hadn't taken much effort.

Kori dried some silverware and put it away, mentally forming her next request. "Would you be willing to pay half of my attorney fees?"

"Absolutely not!"

Her defenses rose and, facing him, she angrily replied, "But it's your fault that I'm in this mess, and I think it's only fair that—"

Brent silenced her by placing a wet finger against her mouth. He narrowed his dark gaze. "I am not going to help you divorce me," he told her quietly, earnestly. "But I will pay for your car to be fixed." He paused, lowering his hand and smiling. "In fact, let's buy you a new one."

"I don't want a new car," Kori muttered irritably. "Just fix my old one."

"What? And make me worry about you all winter, driving that old clunker? I'd rather just buy you a new car that's dependable and has a warranty."

Kori opened her mouth to refuse, but then thought better of it. In fact, she decided she'd have to be nuts not to take the offer. A new car—she'd love a new car!

"You really want to buy me a new car?" she asked as disbelief reared its ugly head. "Oh, you probably mean a new *used* car, right? That is, it will be used by someone else but new to me."

"No, I mean something right off the showroom floor." Brent smiled. "It's the least I can do for you, Kori."

She chewed the corner of her lower lip and gazed at Brent speculatively. This man was most definitely not the same Brent McDonald she once knew. And yet, he was the same man outwardly. The same dark hair, handsome grin. . .and then the same dark gaze looked into her eyes, causing Kori's heart to beat a little faster.

"So, are you two getting along?" Clair asked. She had come into the kitchen unannounced and now stood by the stove with arms folded in front of her. "Or are you guys getting ready for a showdown?"

Brent grinned, his gaze never leaving Kori. "No showdown here."

"Well, the way you're looking at each other," Clair said sarcastically, "I thought either you're in love or someone's going to die."

I think someone's going to die, Kori thought, tearing her gaze from Brent's and picking up another dish to dry. *It might just kill me to be his friend.*

❧

The next morning, Kori slipped out of the apartment before either Clair or Dana awoke. Brent had promised to pick her up early so they could go shopping for a car, and Kori wasn't up to any funny remarks from her sister and roommate. After Brent had left last night, they had teased her mercilessly.

"That man is after you, Kori," Clair had said. She looked at Dana. "He sends her roses, makes her favorite meal, looks at her with moon-eyes. . ." Clair chuckled. "Sounds like love to me."

"Better tell Jared he's got stiff competition," Dana had advised, wearing a silly smile.

"There is no competition," Kori had tried to explain. "Brent is soon to be my ex-husband and then I'm going to marry Jared."

"I think you need your head examined," Clair muttered without a trace of humor.

"And I think you need to mind your own business, big sister!"

After that, things had grown tense and, this morning, Kori still regretted losing her temper. But Kori thought that Clair, of all people, should remember the pain Brent had inflicted upon her when he said he didn't love her anymore. So what if he sent her flowers, cooked her favorite meal, and looked at her with "moon-eyes?" Was that really love? And what was stopping Brent from changing his mind again? He always changed his mind.

Standing outside the apartment complex in the cold November sunshine, Kori wondered if Brent had changed his mind about picking her up this morning. He was late. But then she remembered that Brent's "on time" was always fifteen minutes late. *Looks like he's not such a new man after all,* she mused sarcastically.

Kori sat down on the front cement stairs and waited. . .and thought. . .and waited some more. A person could do a lot of thinking in fifteen minutes, she soon decided. The brisk air seemed to help clear her head and by the time Brent pulled into the parking lot, Kori felt ready to face him.

"Good morning!" Brent said as she climbed into his truck. He looked bright and happy.

"Good morning," Kori replied, though her greeting wasn't as exuberant.

"You think we could eat breakfast before we shop for cars?" Brent asked. "I'm starving."

"Sure."

Brent's next stop was the Forum Family Restaurant, which was just beginning its breakfast rush. Kori and Brent managed to find a table anyway and within moments, coffee and menus arrived.

"Do you have any idea what kind of car you want?" Brent asked while scanning the menu.

"Not really. Something practical, I guess."

Brent grinned at her from over the menu. "What? You don't want a sporty little Porsche?"

Kori had to smile as she shook her head. She debated momentarily whether to tell him about her future plans, but then honesty won out.

"Brent, within the next few years, I want a family. Children. So I want the car I buy today to be something accommodating. I mean, I'll probably have this car for a long time."

Brent nodded speculatively. Then he put down his menu, giving her his full attention.

"And I was thinking before you picked me up this morning," Kori continued. "Well, I just want you to know that I appreciate your willingness to help me this way, but it won't change anything. You're still just a friend and I'm still going to marry Jared."

Brent grinned wryly. "And what's Jared going to say when you show up with a new car? Are you going to tell him 'a friend' bought it for you?"

"No," Kori replied at once. "I'm going to tell him it was part of my divorce settlement."

Brent looked thoroughly amused. "You figured that much out already, huh?"

"I couldn't sleep last night until I did," Kori muttered.

Brent chuckled in spite of himself and then the waitress came and took their orders. After she left, he looked over at Kori and sipped his coffee. "So, how did you and Jared meet, anyway?"

Kori looked back at him, surprised. "You really want to know?"

He shrugged, but his expression was solemn. "Look, Kori, I'll admit that I'm jealous you want him and not me. But I've committed myself to being your friend. . .and what do friends do? They share information about themselves so that they can get to know each other better." He took another sip of his coffee. "That's why I'm asking. I want to get to know you better."

Kori looked sadly into her coffee cup. "You used to know me better than anyone in the whole world." When Brent didn't reply, she forced herself to look up at him.

"Kori, I know I've said them before, and I know they're just words, but they're all I've got: *I'm sorry.*"

She nodded. And she believed that Brent was really sorry. However, Kori had felt a pain that cut so deeply, "sorry" would never, ever heal it. But real love would—and that's what Kori was sure she'd find if she married Jared.

"We met at a picnic last summer," she blurted.

"Last summer?" Brent paused, taking another sip of coffee. "You haven't known the guy very long and now you're ready to marry him? After just a few months? We dated for two years before you agreed to marry me."

"My mistake," Kori said sarcastically, her defenses on the rise.

Brent put down his coffee cup, took off his glasses, and then rubbed his eyes wearily.

Kori sighed, wishing she had not verbally lashed out at him like that. "Look, Brent, this isn't going to work," she said at last. "Let's just forget this car thing and you can take me home. I'll manage. I always manage. I shouldn't have asked for your help."

"Yes, you should have, and, no, let's not forget it." Brent was the one to sigh this time. "I'm struggling, Kori," he confessed in a soft tone of voice. "The Bible says that love suffers long and does not envy. Well, I'm envious. . .of Jared! And I'm not being very patient. I'm reacting out of jealousy."

"The Bible?"

Brent nodded. "It's like a Christian's instruction book on how to live, and I don't seem to be following it very well."

Kori immediately thought of Ryan Carlson and his code of ethics. She admired the man and had often wished that Jared would act toward her the way Ryan behaved toward his girlfriend, Stacie. Gallant and patient. . .

"I'm apologizing again, Kori," Brent said, breaking into her thoughts. "I'm sorry. Truly, deeply sorry."

"I'm sorry, too," she replied. "I shouldn't have gotten so defensive."

Reaching across the table, Brent covered her hand with his. "Truce?"

Kori smiled. "Truce."

Breakfast was served and the conversation stayed light and friendly. Afterwards, they left the restaurant and visited two car dealers. Kori managed to decided on the type of car she'd like—a sporty station wagon. Brent wanted to buy her something more expensive, more trendy, but Kori imagined how convenient a little station wagon would be for grocery shopping and hauling portable cribs and strollers. And the best part of the vehicle, in Kori's mind, was that either side of the backseat could convert into a child's car seat.

"Mark told me about one other dealership," Brent said as they climbed back into his truck. "It's in Menomonee Falls—near the apartment I'm subleasing."

It was the last stop and had the most reasonable prices. Moreover, the salesman went to the same church Brent was attending and knew Mark Henley, Julia McGowan, his fiancée, and Ryan Carlson. Whether or not that was the reason, the salesman gave Brent a great deal on the "little red wagon," as Brent decided to call it.

The papers were signed and Brent paid in full, much to the delight of the car salesman. "You can take delivery by the end of the week," he promised.

Leaving the dealership, Brent offered to drive Kori to and from work this week.

"You've done so much already," she protested. "I don't want you to go out of your way like that."

"Kori, I've got no other plans. Driving you to work and back will give me something to do this week."

She chuckled softly as Brent unlocked the truck's door for her. She climbed in and Brent walked around to the other side.

"So, where to?" he asked, putting the key in the ignition.

Kori shrugged. "Home, I guess."

"Do you have plans with Jared tonight?" Brent asked. He quickly added, "I'm not trying to be nosy. I just wanted to know if you have to be home at a certain time."

Kori shook her head. "Jared is deer hunting."

"Oh?" Brent cranked the engine and pulled his truck out of the dealership's parking lot. "He's a hunter, huh?"

"Yep. He's a hunter, bowler, dart-thrower, baseball and basketball player, an avid Green Bay Packer fan, a true cheese-head, and couch potato."

Brent laughed heartily. "So what does Jared do in his spare time?"

Kori smiled. "He doesn't have any spare time."

"He makes time for you, doesn't he?"

"Of course," Kori replied, wishing she could think of a few more instances when he had.

"Are you a bowler, dart-thrower. . .all those things now, too?"

"Sometimes."

"And other times?"

Kori shrugged. "Other times Jared and I just do our own things."

"Separately?"

She nodded. "Uh-huh."

Brent paused. "Are you and Jared good friends?"

Kori actually had to think about that one for several moments. "No," she finally replied in all honesty. "Jared and I have a different relationship than he has with his buddies, and that's fine because I don't want to be *one of the guys*. I want to be his wife."

"I want my wife to be my best friend," Brent stated off-handedly, and Kori didn't think there was an underlying meaning in his words. He was too preoccupied with his driving.

"Well, maybe someday when you find the right woman, she will be your best friend."

Brent nodded. "Yeah, maybe someday."

Much to her surprise, Kori felt a stab of jealousy. Brent and "the right woman." How would she feel if Brent actually did marry someone else? Would she be hurt all over again? And how ridiculous of her to even contemplate such things, seeing as she was marrying Jared!

Suddenly, Kori understood Brent's "struggling," as he said at breakfast this morning. Emotions could certainly overrule common sense at times!

"Hey," Brent said, changing the subject, "would it be okay if we stopped by my place before I take you home? Remember I told you that my mother moved? Well, I had boxes stored at her house from when I emptied our apartment. . .after you left. I brought them with me to Milwaukee."

"Why did you do that?" Kori asked, amazed.

Brent chuckled. "I didn't really do it intentionally. I had forgotten all about them, but when I stopped to say good-bye to Mom the day I left for Wisconsin, she reminded me and, on a whim, I packed them into my truck." He paused. "I think we should go over their contents so I know what to save and what to throw out."

"Sure," Kori replied, though she couldn't think of anything worth saving from their apartment.

The day she had decided to move to Wisconsin, she had packed her clothes, jewelry, and other personal items, but she had left the rest. Their wedding photo album, framed pictures, knickknacks. . .even her needlepoint on the walls. She left the pots and pans, towels, sheets, pillows, and all the furniture. Then, from the airport, she had phoned Brent and told him he'd have to clean up the apartment if he wanted the security deposit back.

"What did you pack, Brent?" she had to ask. Surely, he didn't pack everything.

He shrugged. "I can't really remember, but I've got four large boxes of stuff. I barely fit them in the back of my truck."

Kori wondered over the wisdom of sorting through these items with Brent. It might stir up more hurt than she could handle. However, Kori soon decided that declaring the things they shared as "garbage" and then seeing them thrown away for good, might be just the thing she needed to do. She'd clean her heart of Brent in preparation for a life with Jared. Out with the old, in with the new—wasn't that how the saying went?

nine

The apartment Brent was subleasing was a modern bi-level with its own entrances. He showed Kori through the front door and then helped her off with her coat. He hung it on the wooden coat stand, then shrugged off his jacket, hanging it up too.

"The living room is this way," he said, leading her up seven carpeted steps.

"This is more spacious than my apartment," she observed.

Brent nodded. "It's spacious and more comfortable than a long-stay hotel would have been. I'm grateful Mark was able to get this for me. Would you like something to drink?"

Kori shrugged and followed Brent into the kitchen. He opened the refrigerator, revealing cans of ginger ale. Brent had never been fond of colas. He pulled two off the top shelf of the nearly empty refrigerator and handed one to her.

She popped the top. "Jared's fridge is full of beer," she stated offhandedly. Then, too late, she wished she hadn't said anything.

"He's not a problem drinker, is he?"

Kori shook her head. "No, just a fun-loving guy. He can handle his alcohol."

"Hmm. . ." Brent took a long drink of his ginger ale. "Well, come on into the living room and I'll show you those boxes I was talking about."

Again, Kori followed Brent to the four brown cardboard boxes that stood in the farthest corner of the living room.

"How 'bout I make a fire?" he asked, hunkering down by the built-in brick fireplace.

"Sure," Kori said with a noncommittal shrug. "Which box should we start on?"

"Doesn't matter."

She set down her ginger ale and opened the box closest to her. "Oh, Brent," she said, laughing, "you didn't have to pack the toilet paper." She pulled out a half-used roll.

Brent chuckled. "I guess I wasn't being particular in my packing."

"I guess," Kori quipped, pulling out a bar of old soap and a couple of threadbare bath towels. "We were so poor," she stated on a melancholy note, fingering the towels. "I bought most of what we had at rummage sales."

"I wasn't very appreciative of all you did back then, Kori. But I am now. Really." Brent shrugged. "Hindsight. . .you know the rest."

Kori just nodded and pulled out a roll of paper towels. Then came two plastic place mats, some cooking utensils, plates, and a toaster. "Oh, Brent," she said, shaking her head pathetically and looking into the very bottom of the box.

Brent peered inside. "Oh, yeah, and I just dumped out the kitchen drawers."

Kori repacked the box. "Garbage. All of it."

"You sure?"

"Positive."

"Okay, I'll take it to the dumpster out back."

Kori sat down on the floor, her back up against the sofa, and began to unpack the next box. It contained all the pictures they'd had on the walls of their apartment.

"Garbage," she said.

"Really?" Brent pulled out one of the framed needlepoint prints Kori had made. It was the one that read "Home Is Where You Hang Your Heart" and it had hearts and flowers in the background. "None of this is worth saving?"

Kori shook her head. "I don't want any reminders of our life together, Brent," she said tersely. "That's why I left all this stuff in California in the first place."

"Okay, fine," he said defensively. Then he carelessly tossed the picture back into the box.

Walking over to the fireplace, Brent stood with his back to Kori and stoked the fire he'd created only moments ago. Oh! but she made him angry. Couldn't she just be nice? They'd had many, many good years together. Why couldn't Kori remember them instead of focusing on their last six months together? Brent knew he'd hurt her badly, but he had apologized at least a dozen times. What more could he do?

Love her, Brent, that still small voice seemed to whisper. *Love never fails.*

"I'd better get going," Kori said, causing Brent to turn around. She stood to her feet. "I'll take a cab if you don't want to drive me home."

Brent sighed in resignation, his inner struggle ceased. "I'll take you home, Kori," he said, "but I wish you'd stay."

She shook her head stubbornly. "You're mad at me. I can tell."

"I'm mad at myself, Kori," Brent said honestly. "If I hadn't been so selfish two and a half years ago, we'd still be happily married."

"Married, maybe," Kori retorted, "but I don't know about the 'happily' part. I mean, you told me when you left me that you weren't ever happy. You said that was the problem."

Brent closed his eyes against a wave of pain and anger. They were hurtful words and, yes, he had said them. But how many times was Kori going to fling them in his face?

"Want to take me home now?" she asked saucily.

Brent opened his eyes and saw Kori's victorious expression. Then he couldn't help a grin. "So you think that if you make me angry enough or hurt my feelings enough I'll turn tail and run back to California, huh?" His grin grew into a full smile. "Guess again, lady."

Kori narrowed her gaze, scrutinizing him, though a little smile played upon her lips.

"And I'm not going to fight with you either," Brent added.

"You're just no fun at all," she teased him. Then she grabbed her can of ginger ale and sat down on the carpeted floor by the fire. Her back was against the sofa. It seemed that Kori had somehow been defused. She was staying.

Brent sighed, feeling a bit weary from his second major challenge of the day. The first had been their sparring at breakfast, and Brent wondered how long he could keep this up. He knew it was God who kept his patience intact, for Brent McDonald knew that he, by nature, was not a patient man.

He sat down beside Kori, his can of ginger ale in hand. "Do you have plans tonight?" he asked.

"You asked me that already," she said right back, sounding defensive. "Why do you want to know?"

"I was just wanted to make sure because if you don't have to go home, I'd sort of like to order some food." Brent grinned. "I'm hungry."

Her features softened. "No, I don't have to be home and. . . Chinese food sounds good."

"Chinese it is," Brent said, delighted that he could have Kori with him that much longer. He looked at his watch. "I'll go pick it up in about an hour and bring it back here. What do you say?"

Kori shrugged. "Okay."

A long moment of silence passed between them as the fire crackled in the brick fireplace. Brent shifted and moved a little closer to Kori. He couldn't help it. She looked so soft and huggable sitting here beside him by the fire.

Kori didn't seem to notice that Brent had moved. "Sometimes I go out with my friends at the clinic. But that's usually on Friday nights. Saturday nights I reserve for Jared, but, as I told you before, Jared went deer hunting."

"Oh, yeah, that's right."

"He was angry when he left, too." She gave Brent a pointed look. "Which is your fault, I might add."

"Mine?"

"Yes, yours—and don't give me that innocent, sweet pout of yours, either."

"I do not pout!" Brent declared.

"Yes, you do. Just ask your mom. You got out of a lot of trouble as a kid by giving her that same look."

Brent laughed. "Okay, I guess I have heard that before." He paused. "But tell me, why was Jared angry?"

"You really want to know? You don't mind me talking about him?"

"We're friends, remember?"

Kori nodded. "Well, it's simple, really. Jared wasn't exactly thrilled to learn that I'm still married." She forced herself not to cringe at the understatement.

"You told him, huh?"

She nodded. "He was pretty upset."

Brent didn't reply, but he thought that was to Jared's credit. Some guys wouldn't care if a woman was married.

Brent put his arm up along the top of the couch, resting it in back of Kori. Then, impulsively, he touched her hair. She was wearing it down today, only the sides were pulled up and secured at the top with a plain, gold barrette. Her golden hair was still as soft as he remembered.

Amazingly, Kori didn't protest his touch, so Brent let his hand get lost in her soft thick tresses, just the way he used to.

"Uhm, you shouldn't be doing this, you know," she chided him half-heartedly. "But I've got to admit, it feels so good." She paused, momentarily thoughtful. "I suppose I shouldn't be enjoying this either, should I?"

Brent smiled. Kori had always loved it when he ran his fingers through her hair. She used to say it relaxed her, and she looked pretty relaxed right now.

"Do you know that Jared never touches my hair like this? Once I even asked him to, but he said he wasn't that sort of a guy."

"Hmm. . ." Brent was glad to hear that.

"Jared isn't very romantic," Kori offered. "He doesn't like to hold hands or have candlelight dinners."

"We used to eat by candlelight a lot."

Kori laughed. "Yeah, our cheap TV dinners by candlelight."

Brent laughed, too. "Ah, but they were romantic."

Kori nodded. "That's one thing about you, Brent. You're a romantic."

"Thanks. . .I think." He lifted a brow. "That was a compliment, wasn't it?"

Kori laughed again. "Yes, it was."

Brent continued to weave his fingers in and out of Kori's long hair, wondering what kind of relationship she had with Jared. She'd already said that he wasn't a romantic guy. He didn't hold Kori's hand or touch her hair. But were they intimate lovers? Brent knew that, biblically, he could go along with the divorce under those circumstances, if his wife was now physically intimate with another man; however, he almost didn't think it mattered, not to his heart. And that's when he realized just how much he loved his wife. He would gladly take her back regardless of where she'd been, though he suspected she hadn't "been" anywhere.

"In case you're wondering, I never slept with Jared," Kori suddenly blurted.

Brent lifted his brows, surprised by her sudden candidness.

"I don't know why I'm even telling you this," she continued, "except I can practically *hear* the question rolling around in your head! I mean, it's none of your business and maybe you don't even care—"

"I care very much, Kori." Brent gave her a gentle smile. "And we still know each other very well, don't we?"

Kori shrugged and a sudden silence grew between them. Brent sensed that she was wondering the same thing about him. At one time, they'd been so close they used to think alike.

"I haven't been intimate with anyone else either," he told her. "But I will confess to giving Meg a good-night kiss after a couple of dates. It never went any further, though, and I never dated anyone else. I didn't have time. My dad got sick and I was working a lot of hours, so I was forced to put my social life on hold." Brent smiled. "Then I was born-again the Bible way, and now I see those circumstances as part of the providential hand of God. Even though I didn't know I was still married, God did."

Kori turned pensive for several long moments. Her head was turned away from him and Brent thought she was watching the fire.

"What are you thinking about?" he finally asked.

"I was thinking that. . .well, I've kissed Jared a lot and here all along I've been married." She shook her head and looked back at Brent. "That doesn't make me feel very good about myself."

"But you didn't know, Kori. You aren't responsible for something you didn't know."

She nodded, but Brent could tell by the little frown of concern marring her forehead that she wasn't at all relieved by his statement. Kori always did have a good conscience. She had always been a good person, unwilling to hurt anyone.

"I couldn't bring myself to kiss Jared last week," she finally said. "I think that's what really made him mad—the fact that I wouldn't kiss him."

"Understandable, at least from his standpoint."

"Oh, what am I going to do?" she muttered forlornly, pulling her knees up to her chin. Then she wrapped her arms around them.

"You want me to answer that question?" Brent asked facetiously.

"No," Kori replied emphatically, "because I know what you'd say. You'd say I should stay married to you and forget Jared."

Brent nodded. "That's exactly what I'd say."

"Well, I won't." Kori moved away from him in one, sudden move and stood up. "If I stayed married to you, Brent, you'd probably come home one day and announce that God told you to be a medical missionary in the Amazon or something. You'd make me pack my bags and away we'd go."

Brent chuckled.

"Well, no way," Kori said seriously, though she had a

smile in her eyes. "I've chased enough rainbows with you. Now I want stability. I want a house. . .a home. I want children." She paused. "And I guess I want children more than anything else."

Brent took a moment to consider her statement. "And what would happen if you married Jared," he challenged her, "and then discovered you couldn't have children with him because of any number of medical reasons?"

Kori's green eyes widened. Obviously she hadn't thought of that.

The phone rang and Brent got up to answer it. "Oh, hi, Dana. Yeah, she's here." He held out the phone to Kori. "For you."

She frowned curiously but took the portable phone. "How did you know I was here and how did you get Brent's phone number?"

"He only left a hundred messages for you last week," Dana replied facetiously. "I got his number off one of them and I had a hunch you two were still together. Did you buy a car?"

"Yep. It's a small-size station wagon."

"Station wagon? Whose idea was it to buy that?"

"Mine. I wanted a family car."

"Oh." Dana paused. "So what are you guys doing over there?"

"Just talking."

"Sure you are."

Kori rolled her eyes. She wasn't up to her roommate's teasing at the moment. "What can I do for you, Dana?"

"I wondered if I could borrow your lilac-colored sweater tonight. I promise I'll take good care of it, and then I'll have it dry-cleaned when I'm done borrowing it."

"Sure, go ahead."

"Clair and I are going out tonight. She got invited to a party and I'm going to have dinner with a friend from high school."

"Okay. I'll see you guys whenever."

"Oh, and Jared called."

"He did? Is he home?"

"Nope. He said he was calling from the lodge, whatever that means. Anyway, he was kind of mad that you weren't home."

"Did you tell him where I was?"

"No way, Kori. You know me better than that. You, Clair, and I are like the Three Musketeers. One for all and all for one."

"Yeah, something like that," Kori replied with a little laugh. "So what did you tell him?"

"Jared? Oh, I said I thought you were shopping so he said he'd call back later tonight."

"Really?" Kori wondered if something serious had happened. Why else would Jared call her from deer hunting with the guys? "Well, thanks, Dana, and I'll talk to you later."

Kori shut off the telephone. Then, leaving the living room, she found Brent in the kitchen, busily paging through the phone book.

"I'm trying to find a Chinese restaurant that's close by," he explained.

"There's a good one near my apartment. We could just eat there or take the food to my place."

"Okay, let's decide when we get to the restaurant. I'm hungry."

As she left with Brent, Kori never felt so torn in two in all her life. She had every intention of marrying Jared and yet she had enjoyed so much her fireside chat with Brent this afternoon. She had talked to him in a way that she could never talk to Jared. Furthermore, she had enjoyed Brent's touch and the way he sat so close to her.

But Brent McDonald could charm the birds out of the trees, Kori reminded herself. *I cannot succumb to his charm. We're just friends,* she admonished herself. *Friends and nothing more!*

ten

Letting herself into the apartment complex, Kori stood in the lobby and watched Brent drive off. They'd had an enjoyable dinner at a small Chinese restaurant and, in a way, Kori was sorry to see the evening come to an end. It galled her to admit it, but she liked Brent's company. She always had.

Taking the elevator up to her apartment, Kori opened the door and walked into the front hallway. The empty darkness reminded her that Clair and Dana were out for the night. Kori went on into the living room, turned on a lamp, and then headed for her bedroom and changed into a long nightshirt. By the time she reentered the living room, the telephone was ringing.

"Hi, honey," Jared said on the other end. "I've been trying to get you all night. Where have you been?"

"Out with a friend," she replied easily.

"Oh, yeah? Who?"

Kori paused, wondering what Jared would think of her friendship with Brent. *He probably wouldn't like it,* she decided. *Better not tell him.* "It's no one you know," she finally replied, though her conscience pricked her for avoiding the truth.

"Oh." Jared paused. "I thought maybe you were with Joan or Cathy. . .you're still going to the Deer Hunter Widows' Ball with them on Thanksgiving Day, right?"

"Right," Kori said, glad that she could state the truth now. She, Joan, and Cathy had been planning to attend "the ball" for months.

"Sue and Bonnie are going too."

"Oh, good," Kori said. The women were wives of Jared's "buddies" and the ball was being held at a local tavern, run by one of Jared's cousins. A radio station was even going to be there, playing music all night.

"Listen, honey, the reason I'm calling is. . .well, I just wanted to tell you I'm sorry for getting so bent out of shape when you told me about your situation. It took me by surprise and I guess I sort of overreacted. But I was talking to some of the guys last night, and I realized that this isn't really such a big deal after all. You get a divorce and it's over. We get married."

"That was my plan," Kori said, wishing she didn't sound so timid. Yes! It still was her plan. Nothing had changed. So what if she and Brent were friends? She stiffened with new resolve.

"You know," Jared continued, "you could move in with me while all this divorce business is going on."

"No, Jared, I don't think—"

"Don't say no, Kori. Just think it over again. If you say you'll move in with me, we'll take that cruise in February like we planned. Just won't get married, that's all. And so what's the big deal? Lots of people don't get married."

"I know, but. . ."

"Well, at least think about it. Reconsider, Kori."

She sighed in resignation. . .for now. However, she knew she would never accept such a proposition. Kori wanted a commitment that would last forever. This was her second time around with marriage and, for her, it would be the last time around. Her heart couldn't take anymore.

"I also realized," Jared was saying, "that your ex-husband . . .or whatever he is, can't sue me. I mean, it's a free country, and it's not like there are kids involved."

"No," Kori murmured, "there are no kids involved." And then it occurred to her. "But you do like kids, don't you, Jared?" They hadn't ever discussed having children before. Kori had only assumed that he would want children as much as she did. She had told him many times that she wanted a family and he'd never balked at the idea.

"Kids are okay," Jared replied. "My friends think they're kind of a burden, though."

"A burden?"

"Yeah. Well, I got to get back to the card game."

"All right." Kori shook off her sudden uneasiness. "Thanks for calling, Jared." She knew it was a big sacrifice for him to take time away from his deer camp buddies and call her. "It's nice to hear your voice again. . .and I'm glad you're not still angry with me."

"No, I'm not. And, Kori? I love you."

Kori's heart felt like it plummeted to her toes. Jared had never spoken words of love to her before. He'd merely insinuated them which, to her, had meant a lot at the time. After all, actions speak louder than words and "I love you" were just words. However, her heart had so longed to hear Jared say them. And now he was. . .yet it troubled her. But why?

"Kori, are you there?"

"Yes, I just. . .well. . .I—"

"Oh, I get it. You can't tell me you love me back 'cause your roommates are standing there listening. That's all right. I understand, honey. I wouldn't want to say 'I love you' if the guys were around."

Kori couldn't seem to choke out a single reply.

"Are you okay?"

"Yes," she said quickly, somehow finding her voice again.

"All right, then. I'm going to hang up."

"Thanks again for calling, Jared," Kori replied, trying to put a smile in her voice. "Good-bye."

Kori placed the telephone receiver back in its cradle. She felt guilty but didn't know why. *I haven't done anything wrong,* she mused. But then she remembered how Brent had run his fingers through her hair that afternoon and how good it felt. She remembered that she hadn't stopped him and how much she'd liked it. What would Jared say if he found out? Had she betrayed him?

Maybe I shouldn't be friends with Brent, she thought.

However, the idea of having no more contact with him wasn't at all appealing. After today, Kori felt like a part of her had been opened to the fresh air again after a long, dark hibernation. She could talk to Brent. He understood her. She didn't want to sever their relationship—not anymore.

So what am I going to do? she wondered for the second time today. She knew what Brent would tell her. She knew what Jared would tell her. She even knew what Clair would tell her. But what did her heart tell her?

Kori just didn't know.

⅋

The next day, Kori was up early. She'd had trouble sleeping, and by 6:30, she abandoned the idea of sleep altogether.

Walking into the kitchen, Kori made a pot of coffee. Then she decided to make an elaborate breakfast for her roommates. Blueberry muffins, bacon, and eggs.

"What smells so good?" Dana asked, coming out of her bedroom. She yawned and stretched, still looking sleepy. "I wanted to sleep in today, Kori," she complained, "but my stomach started growling when I smelled the bacon frying."

Kori smiled. "Will you join me for breakfast?"

"Sure."

Clair woke up next. She was never one to stay in bed past 7:30. During the week, Clair was the first one up at five o'clock, and she was out of the apartment by seven. Therefore, sleeping until 7:30 was a luxury for her.

"Coffee?" Kori asked her older sister.

"You bet."

Kori poured the hot, steamy brew and then dished up breakfast and they all sat down.

"Did you and Brent have fun yesterday?" Clair asked.

"I don't know about 'fun,' but Brent and I had a nice day together, yes. And, Clair, I'm sorry for losing my temper with you Friday night." Kori shook her head, feeling confused all over again. "I enjoyed being with Brent yesterday. . .maybe I do need my head examined."

Clair smiled. "Are you still in love with him, Kori?"

"No! Of course not!" She paused, setting down her fork and then relented. "Oh, I don't know how I feel about Brent." Then she murmured, "I don't know what love is anymore."

"Ah, the age-old question: What is love?" Dana laughed softly. "You know what I think love is? Love means never having to say you're sorry."

"Thank you very much, Erich Segal," Clair quipped and they all began to laugh.

"Oh, sorry," Dana said between giggles, "I just watched that movie, *Love Story,* on The Late, Late Show, and you know how much I like old flicks."

"I wish my dilemma could be solved as easily as an old movie," Kori remarked.

"It's really a no-brainer, Kori," Clair told her. "I mean, Brent is a changed man, he's still in love with you and wants to give your marriage another go, and. . .and you are, after all, still married."

"But you don't understand," Kori said softly, as if pleading her case. "I told Jared I'd marry him because I thought Brent and I were divorced. In essence, I don't feel married to Brent, I feel engaged to Jared."

"Then you're in love with Jared, right?" Dana asked.

"I. . .I don't know."

"Well, that's what you've got to figure out, Kori," Clair advised. "Who are you in love with?"

"But what is love?"

"It's that warm, fuzzy feeling you get when you're with someone special," Dana told her.

"Warm and fuzzy?" Kori had never experienced "warm and fuzzy" with Jared. But she had with Brent. Once, she'd been so in love with Brent she couldn't see straight.

"Love is responsibility and commitment," Clair said logically. "If you love someone, you make time for him. You make him your responsibility. Not that you're responsible for his happiness or for what he does or doesn't do, but you take care of his needs." She shrugged. "That's what marriage is all about and, after I marry Zach, I'll take care of him. Like sewing the button back on his pants, making his meals, washing his dirty socks." Clair paused and smiled. "Now *that's* love!"

"But I did all that for Brent and it didn't matter," Kori protested. "He still left me."

"And, just like I said, you're not responsible for what Brent does or doesn't do. Don't you see, Kori? You did right, Brent did wrong," Clair replied. "But now he wants a second chance."

"Are you going to give him another chance, Kori?" Dana asked.

"No!" she said, getting up from the table. "I'm going to marry Jared. Nothing has changed. Brent and I can only be friends." She shook her head as if to clear it. "Look, you guys. When I even begin to consider giving Brent another chance, I hear his voice saying, 'I just don't love you anymore.' That's what he told me when I suggested a second chance at our marriage—before I left California, and I was devastated." She turned to her sister. "Clair, you know how devastated I was."

"I know."

"Dana, you remember."

She nodded. "I remember."

"So? What do I do?" Kori picked up her empty plate and dirty silverware and walked to the kitchen. She rinsed her dishes and left them in the sink for later.

"I guess what you do depends on how you feel," Clair advised, coming into the kitchen behind Kori. "If you feel like you're still in love with Brent, give him another chance. If not, divorce him and marry Jared. It's simple."

Kori nodded. Simple—oh! how she wished it were. If only she wasn't so emotional and introspective. If only she could be practical like Clair.

eleven

Brent was on time to pick up Kori for work on Monday morning and she was amazed. She had thought for sure he'd be his usual fifteen minutes late. She had even called her manager to let her know she'd be late.

"I guess I've had to learn to be on time," Brent said with a chuckle when Kori mentioned it. He glanced her way. "Did you have a good day yesterday?"

Kori nodded. "Didn't do a whole lot. Read the newspaper, did some grocery shopping with Dana, washed some clothes. The usual, I guess. How 'bout you?"

"I went to church in the morning and had lunch with Mark Henley, his fiancée Julia, and some of her family. Then I went back to church and didn't get home till about nine o'clock."

"That's a lot of church," Kori remarked, wearing a curious frown. "Isn't it boring to sit in church that long?"

Brent grinned. "It's only boring if the pastor's delivery is boring, I guess. But the pastor yesterday spoke in a way that made the Bible come alive for me and I was able to apply the spiritual truths to my life."

"Like what?"

Brent thought for a moment. "Like going to the Lord with my problems and trusting Him to take care of them instead of trying to handle them on my own. Yesterday I was reminded that God's ways are perfect, mine aren't."

"Hmm. . ." Kori didn't know what to make of Brent's comments except, she thought, they sounded a lot like Ryan Carlson's. At first, when Ryan used to talk about his dependence upon God, Kori thought it was a sign of weakness. Now, however, she wasn't so sure. Ryan didn't seem weak at ll. He seemed like he had his life together while hers was falling to pieces.

Minutes later, Brent pulled into the parking lot of the clinic, and Kori climbed out of his truck. "Have a good day," he told her. "I'll pick you up tonight. About five?"

"Depends on our patients. Better make it 5:30."

"Okay."

Kori smiled at him. "Thanks, Brent. I appreciate the ride."

"Anytime," he replied, smiling back.

Closing the truck's door, Kori waked into the clinic. Already patients were lined up at the front desk and the receptionists looked harried. Diane was explaining an insurance copayment to an unhappy-looking patient, Gigi was scheduling an appointment, and Vicki was in the back, answering the telephone. A sure sign that today would be a busy one.

And it was. Ryan kept Kori so occupied that she barely had time for a lunch break. By six o'clock that evening, they had seen twenty-five patients—and that was just Ryan's practice alone. The other five family practice doctors had seen their share of people as well.

"I hate Mondays," Susie murmured as she worked on completing her route slips.

Kori was finishing up on her own. "I hate Mondays, too." The phone rang. "And this better not be one of the receptionists asking if we'll work in another patient, either!" she declared, picking up the receiver.

"Hi, Kori," Jeanmarie said pleasantly. She was a part-time receptionist. "There's a man down here waiting for you. He's been here for about a half hour. Thought you should know."

"Brent. Oh, no! I forgot about him."

Jeanmarie laughed, her bubbly personality evident even over the telephone line. "What do you want me to tell him?"

"Oh, I don't know," Kori sighed, surveying her paperwork. "I guess I can be done in about fifteen minutes. Ask him if he'll wait."

"Okay." Jeanmarie covered the receiver and Kori heard a series of muffled replies. "Yeah, he says he'll wait."

"Tell him thanks and I'll try to hurry."

Kori hung up the phone and tackled her paperwork again.

"Who's Brent?" Susie asked.

"Just a friend," Kori replied, not even glancing up from her desk.

"Girlfriend," Susie drawled, "you can't be 'just a friend' with a man!"

Kori looked over at her. "Why not?"

"Because it'll never stay just a friendship." Susie shook her head at her. "You'll be telling him your woes one day and he'll feel bad for you and hug you and then a hug will turn into a kiss and then a kiss will lead to—"

"All right, all right. I get the picture. But it's not that way. Brent is. . .well, he's my ex-husband, okay?"

Susie's brows shot up in surprise. "Oh? Do tell."

Kori went back to her paperwork, refusing to elaborate on the situation. "Ex-husband" was as detailed a description as her coworkers were going to get at this point.

"What does Jared say about you being friends with your ex?"

"Nothing," Kori replied honestly.

"Nothing?" When Kori didn't answer, Susie continued. "Does that mean he doesn't know?"

"He knows about Brent," Kori muttered, wishing Susie weren't so inquisitive. And yet, they had been good friends for the last year. They talked about everything going on in their lives. Kori knew about Susie's children and about her mother who had diabetes and about her brother who was getting married in the spring of next year. And Susie knew about Clair and Dana. She knew that Kori was divorced and was now engaged to Jared. It made sense that Susie would be confused by Kori's reticence.

However, she just didn't want to talk about it—maybe because she wasn't comfortable with her situation yet. It still wasn't resolved by any stretch of the imagination. And maybe Susie was right: maybe she would end up getting too close to Brent if their friendship continued.

Then, as if to affirm her suspicions, Kori remembered how he had stroked her hair last Saturday afternoon and she remembered how much she had liked it. . .

Kori suddenly felt a pair of strong hands on her shoulders and snapped out of her reverie. Turning, she was surprised to find the object of her thoughts standing over her. "How did you get up here?"

"I just saw Ryan in the lobby and he pointed out the way," Brent answered.

"Oh." Kori looked at Susie who was watching her expectantly, so she began introductions at once.

"Nice to meet you, Brent," Susie said assertively. Then she leaned back in her chair, crossed her arms, and considered Brent thoughtfully. "I'll bet you're the guy who sent Kori those roses last week."

He nodded. "That was me." Brent reached over Kori's shoulder and took a picture off her bulletin board. "So this must be Jared, huh?"

"Yes," Kori replied, stacking up her charts for tomorrow. She stood then and prepared to leave while Brent replaced the picture.

"Well, I don't know about Jared," he said, grinning mischievously, "but that fish he's holding looks like a great catch."

Susie grinned and turned back to her paperwork.

"Jared is a 'great catch,' too," Kori told Brent. "Are you ready to go?"

He nodded. "Just waiting for you."

They left the clinic and walked through the lot to where Brent had parked his truck. He opened the door for Kori and she climbed in. After Brent was seated and cranked the engine, Kori apologized for being so late.

"Hey, no problem," he said easily. Brent glanced her way and gave her a smile. "But now you've got to make dinner for me."

"What?"

"All that waiting made me hungry. I only ate a bowl of cereal this morning."

"Well, drop me off and then you can stop at Burger King on your way home."

"But I'm sick of fast food," he said pitifully, "and I'm sick of eating in restaurants. I want an old-fashioned, home-cooked meal, Kori. Wouldn't you make that for me?" He added sweetly, "I waited over an hour for you."

Kori rolled her eyes, hating that Brent could tug on her heartstrings this way.

"I was thinking of meat loaf," he continued.

"I'm sure you were," she retorted, knowing meat loaf was one of Brent's favorite dishes—at least it had been, before he decided to become a vegetarian. But he had changed his mind about food, just like he changed his mind about everything else.

Brent stopped at a red light. "What do you say, Kori? There's a grocery store right here. I'll pay for everything if you'll agree to cook. We'll go over to my place and while we're waiting for dinner we can sort through the last two boxes I brought from California."

Kori looked over at him. "But I'm tired, Brent."

He turned and looked out over the steering wheel. "Okay, if you'll make the meat loaf—because no one can make meat loaf like you—I'll make everything else: mashed potatoes, tossed salad, hot rolls from the oven."

Kori thought about it for a moment and then the light turned green. "Oh, all right," she conceded. "I'll make you a meat loaf." *But it will be the last time,* she added silently. She had suddenly made up her mind that she was going to break off her friendship with Brent. And she would tell him so tonight.

≈

Kori formed the meat and put it into a glass loaf pan. Then, after washing her hands, she slipped it into the oven beside the two large baking potatoes. In the grocery store, Brent had changed his mind from mashed potatoes to baked. Typical.

Brent looked at his watch now. "About an hour till dinner?"

Kori nodded, putting her engagement ring back on her finger. She had taken it off so she could mix the meat loaf with her hands. She looked at it contemplatively, before turning to Brent. "I think we should talk."

"Sure." He leaned casually against the counter. "What's on your mind?"

"Our friendship, for one thing."

"Oh?"

Kori nodded. "At first I thought it was a good thing—us being friends. I thought it would alleviate the animosity I had for you—and it did." She sighed, shaking her head ruefully. "But it's not working out, Brent."

"Why?" The question was spoken softly, curiously, not impatiently or demanding and, once more, Kori marvelled at the change in this man. And yet. . .she was promised to another.

"We're getting too close, Brent."

He smiled. "We're married, Kori. Don't you think it's a good thing if a married couple grows closer?"

Kori was shaking her head vehemently. "No, we're divorced. Maybe not legally. . .yet. But emotionally. . .we're divorced."

Brent paused, looking thoughtful. Then he stepped forward and pulled Kori into his arms. Her first impulse was to push him away, but she couldn't seem to deny herself the feeling of Brent's tender embrace. *It's just a hug,* she told herself. *It's a hug good-bye.*

Brent pulled back. "Kori, I can't make you be my friend and I can't make you love me," he said with his dark brown eyes filled with a sadness that tugged at her heart. "Except," he added, lowering his head, "I think you do."

Brent kissed her softly and all Kori could think about was what Susie had said at work. "A hug will turn into a kiss and a kiss will lead to. . ."

Kori turned her head away, but she was already too late. She had responded to Brent's kiss more than she had wanted.

"I understand your confusion," Brent whispered, "but at least be honest with yourself about how you feel about me. You still love me as much as I love you."

"No!" Kori pushed herself away from him. "It's not love, Brent. It's remembering a time when we shared something *like* love."

Brent narrowed his dark gaze. "*Like* love? What's that supposed to mean?"

"It means we obviously didn't have a *real* love together if it failed."

Brent turned thoughtful again. "You know, Kori," he said at last. "You're right. You are absolutely right."

Kori didn't know how to reply. She couldn't very well argue with him if he was agreeing with her.

"The Bible says 'love never fails.' "

It surprised Kori to learn she agreed with something in the Bible, even though she didn't understand this particular topic at all. She shrugged. "To tell you the truth, Brent, I don't know what love is anymore."

He smiled. "Well, I do. I know what it is now. . .now that I know Jesus Christ." He stepped forward and put his arms back around Kori's waist. "Can I do my best to show you what love is?"

Kori lifted a derisive brow. "I don't think that's love, Brent. I think that's called something else."

He laughed. "No, Kori, I think you misunderstood me. If I were to show you what real love is, it would take me at least. . .oh, the rest of our lives."

Kori stepped out of his embrace. "I haven't got that long. Jared comes home from deer hunting this weekend."

"Then you've got some decisions to make, Kori. Is it going to be him? Or me?"

"A week ago, I would have said 'him,' but now I'm not so sure." She looked over at Brent who was standing there so cool and confident. It angered her. "Can't you see this is tearing me apart?"

Brent smiled wryly. "Indecision will kill you."

"Yeah, and it is."

"Want me to make the decision for you?"

Kori rolled her eyes in silent reply and then walked out of the kitchen. Brent's chuckles echoed behind her.

"Say, Kori," he called, his tone much lighter now, "would you like some flavored coffee or a ginger ale?"

"No," she muttered, sitting down on the sofa in the living room.

"How about a glass of sparkling mineral water?"

"No, thanks."

She spied the two boxes left to rummage through. *May as well get it over with,* she thought, in spite of the fact that she'd deemed it all garbage anyway.

twelve

Kori began to sort through the box and found it contained only miscellaneous items. Nothing worth keeping.

"You can throw all of this out, too, Brent," she told him as he walked into the living room.

"Okay," he replied easily, sitting down on the couch.

On to the fourth and final box of "garbage." Kori began sifting through its contents when suddenly her hand found a wad of tissue paper and, curious, she had to see what was wrapped up inside. It was something heavy, she realized, putting the object in her lap. Slowly, she began to unravel the tissue paper.

"Oh," she breathed once she uncovered the thing. It was a music box in the shape of a carousel. Three pastel-painted, porcelain ponies went up and down and traveled its circumference to the tune of "The Impossible Dream."

Tears stung Kori's eyes as she remembered the melody and then she just had to wind it up. The tinkle-bell tune began and Kori tried to recall the words to the song. How did it go again?

> To dream the impossible dream, to fight the unbeatable foe.
> To bear with unbearable sorrow, to run where the brave dare not go. . .

"That music box was on top of your dresser, wasn't it?" Brent asked.

Kori nodded and swallowed down the lump of emotion suddenly stuck in her throat.

> To right the unrightable wrong, to love pure and chaste from afar.

*To try when your arms are too weary, to reach the
unreachable star!*

"Where did we get that thing, anyway?"

With a sniff and another swallow, Kori replied, "I bought it."

"Oh, yeah? I don't remember."

Kori did. She remembered well. "I used to walk by a novelty shop on the way home from my evening waitress job," she explained, "and every day, I'd see this little carousel in the window. I was so drawn to it.

"Then one night I went into the store to have a better look. The clerk took the music box from out of its display and handed it to me. I wound it up, heard the melody, and it was like I just had to have it. It reminded me of you, Brent. . .it reminded me of us. You were always dreaming the impossible dream and reaching for those unreachable stars. So was I. . ."

Kori paused, fingering the treasured memento. "This was the only music box in the shop of its kind and it cost ninety-five dollars. I fell in love with it, but I knew we didn't have that kind of money. Then the sales clerk told me she'd put it aside for me and I could make payments on it. So that's what I did. Every night when I walked home, I'd stop and put down half my tip money for the music box. Sometimes it was five dollars, sometimes it was twenty, but eventually I paid it off—without sacrificing grocery money or funds to pay the bills—and finally the music box was mine."

Kori wound it up again and gazed at it wistfully. "I always thought I'd give this to our firstborn child. Like a keepsake." She paused and seemed to struggle with her next sentence. "I wanted a baby so badly. . .my impossible dream."

Brent just stared at her. "I never knew. . .Kori, why didn't you ever tell me how deeply you wanted to have a baby?"

She laughed curtly. "With you in medical school, we were scraping just to get by. We couldn't have handled the expense of a child." She sighed and her voice softened. "But I was hoping that once you got done. . ."

Brent didn't know what to say. He didn't think he and Kori had had any secrets between them while they were married. But apparently there were secrets galore. While Brent, in all his selfishness, was dreaming of being a bachelor again, Kori was dreaming of raising a family. Neither one told the other until their dreams blew up in their faces. And now, here they were, trying to put all the pieces back together—at least Brent was trying.

"I wish I would have known," he muttered ruefully.

"What difference would it have made?"

"I don't know. Maybe I would have come to my senses sooner."

"Or maybe," Kori countered, "you would have left me *and* our child." She shook her head adamantly. "No. It's a good thing I didn't have a baby."

Her voice had taken on that hard-sounding tone that Brent was beginning to recognize. Instead of showing her hurt, Kori showed that she was hard. And until he figured out a way to soften her up again, she'd stay hard.

Brent sighed wearily. Three steps forward, two steps back—what kind of progress was he making with Kori, anyway? Would she ever forget the past?

Lord, help me, Brent whispered inwardly in prayer. *This situation is beginning to infuriate me. I don't think I'll ever be sorry enough for Kori. Maybe she's right, this isn't going to work. Maybe there's no hope for us after all.*

Then that still small voice: *Love suffers long. . .love bears all things, believes all things, hopes all things, endures all things. Love never fails.*

With another sigh—but this time one of resolve—Brent watched as Kori wrapped up the musical porcelain carousel and put it back into the box of miscellaneous items. Then she stood. "I don't want any of this stuff, Brent. Throw it out."

He stood as well. "You don't even want the music box?"

"I especially don't want the music box."

Kori looked so hurt that Brent felt sick. "I'm *so sorry,*" he told her, emphatically.

She nodded. "Would you take me home now, please?" Kori practically croaked out the question and Brent saw the tears as they formed in the corners of her light-green eyes and then slipped down her cheeks.

"Kori," he said, coming to her.

"Please," she implored him, holding out a hand as if to forestall him. "Please, I just want to go home."

Brent shook his head. "Kori, I can't let you go now. Not this way."

She put her hands over her face and cried in shoulder-shaking, silent sobs.

"Oh, Kori. . ."

Brent closed the distance between them and put his arms around her, holding her tightly. She didn't fight him but instead sobbed against his shoulder.

"Shhhh, Kori, don't cry," Brent said gently. Then he realized that in all the years they'd been together, he had never seen Kori cry this hard. Oh, he'd seen her tears, tears that were easily brushed aside by his selfishness; however, he'd never heard her sob. Not like this, and in that brief moment, Brent thought he had gotten a glimpse of the enormity of the hurt he'd inflicted on Kori. "Shhh," he repeated, as his hold around her tightened, "don't cry. Please don't cry."

At last her tears subsided and Kori rested her cheek against Brent's shoulder. He held her until her breathing gradually slowed to its normal rhythm.

"Kori," he said, and pushing her back, he cupped her tear-streaked face, "you and I can have lots of babies." Brent smiled down into her eyes.

In spite of herself, Kori smiled.

"That's better," Brent told her, lowering his head so that his nose touched hers affectionately.

She sniffed. "I need to blow my nose."

"By all means."

Kori's misty smile grew.

Brent brought his chin back. "There's a clean towel and washcloth in the bathroom just off of the kitchen. Why don't you go freshen up?"

Kori nodded.

"Then I want to show you something," Brent told her as she started to leave the room. "I think now's a good time."

Again Kori nodded as she made her way to the bathroom. She couldn't believe the way she'd lost control of herself moments ago. Picking up a tissue, Kori gave her nose a healthy blow. Then, looking at the mirror which hung on the wall over the sink, she shook her head in dismay at the red-eyed reflection that stared back. She lifted the washcloth from off the towel rack and began to wash her face. The cold water felt good against her swollen eyes.

As she continued to hold the washcloth against her face, Kori couldn't help but think about what Brent had said: *"You and I can have lots of babies."* Her heart pulled and tugged in every direction. Kori wanted so desperately to have a home and children; but what she yearned for most was a love that would never let her go. She had thought Jared would be the one who would win her heart and love her forever, yet it was Brent whose words and gentle touches spoke to that innermost longing within her.

Kori looked back up at her reflection. Her eyes appeared less puffy and red now. *Should I give Brent another chance?* she wondered. To even consider the question was frightening for Kori. It had taken so long to learn to live without him. Could she really forget the past and give their marriage another go? What if it happened again? On the other hand, Brent certainly seemed like a different man—like he'd learned a valuable lesson. Everyone makes mistakes. . .

A soft knock sounded on the bathroom door. "Kori? Are you okay?"

"Yes, I'm fine," she called back. "I'll be out in a minute."

She took one last glance at her tearstained face and decided it would have to do. She wished she were one of those women who looked beautiful after a good cry, but she wasn't. However, the red blotches were beginning to fade at last.

With a deep, cleansing breath, Kori left the bathroom and met Brent in the living room. He was sitting on the sofa with a stack of photographs in his hand.

He patted the cushion beside him. "Come over here and sit down. I want to show you something."

"No more strolls down Memory Lane, Brent," Kori protested, thinking the pictures were some more of their past. "I can't take any more."

Brent smiled. "No more past, only present and future. Come on. Sit down."

Kori complied.

"Here. Take a look at these."

Kori took the photographs and leafed through them. They were pictures of a house. A red-brick house with white trim and a little white picket fence surrounding the yard.

Kori suddenly paused. "Brent. . .?" Hadn't they always said they'd have a red-brick house with a little white picket fence?

He smiled. "I bought it. It's. . .*our* house."

Kori stared at him, nonplussed.

"It's in Garden Grove, a wonderful little neighborhood just outside of Los Angeles. I closed on it just before I came to Wisconsin."

"You're out of your mind!"

"Very possibly." Brent chuckled and even Kori had to suppress a grin. "Here, look." He took the photos and leaned closer to Kori. "This is the living room. The previous owners painted all the woodwork yellow. It looks hideous, so you've got your work cut out for you, stripping, sanding, and staining."

Kori lifted a brow. "Aren't you being a bit presumptuous?"

"Kori, you're so good with stuff like this. Remember when you refinished that rocking chair for my sister? She still has it in her living room by the fireplace."

Kori remembered that particular project very well. She looked down at the photograph again. "What kind of wood is underneath the yellow paint?" she couldn't help asking.

"Oak—there's oak woodwork throughout the house, including the floors. Here, look." Brent showed her a picture of the dining room with its built-in corner hutch. Then came the picture of the spacious kitchen. "I know you'll want to paint and rewallpaper in here."

Inadvertently, Kori nodded. All she could think of was that the orange flowered paper didn't suit her decorating tastes at all.

"Okay, now look at this." Brent showed her a picture of the back porch, which, he said, was accessible from the landing on the stairwell going up to the second floor. "There's a little deck out here. It faces the west, looks out over the palm trees. You and I can sit out here and watch the sunset."

Kori glanced at him. "Always the romantic, aren't you?"

"Yep. Now look at this." Brent showed her photographs of the bedrooms. Three upstairs and one, the master bedroom, downstairs and, again, Brent's words rang in her ears. *You and I can have lots of babies. . .*

With an audible sigh, Kori dropped her head back against the sofa.

"What's wrong?"

"You're what's wrong. You tempt me beyond imagination." She turned her head toward him and his chocolate-brown eyes locked with hers. His held a question, hers held her heart. "If you really still love me, why didn't you come for me sooner, Brent?" she asked softly.

Forgetting the photographs, he gathered Kori in his arms. "I would have. . .I mean, I wanted to. I just didn't know. . ." Brent tightened his hold as Kori's arms went around him. "I only found out we were still married a couple of months before my father died. My first impulse was to go ahead and file for divorce as I originally planned—mainly because I figured it was too late to do anything else. But then I started thinking—"

"Dreaming," Kori corrected him.

"Yeah, well, once a dreamer, always a dreamer." Brent

placed a kiss on her forehead. "But dreams do come true, you know."

Kori didn't argue. She was too tired and leaning against Brent this way, listening to the sure and steady beat of his heart, made her feel so safe and secure. . .even loved. But was this really love?

Then Brent sat up a little straighter. He cupped Kori's chin with one hand. "Let's give our marriage another chance," he murmured as his lips brushed against hers. "I promise I'll never hurt you again."

Kori turned, pushing herself away from Brent. "I won't say no," she told him in all honesty. "Part of me wants to give our marriage another chance. But I have to think this over. I mean, I don't want to hurt Jared. He says he loves me—just like you do. And whatever I feel for him, it was strong enough to agree to marry him." She paused. "I need to sort out my feelings. I need time."

Brent didn't reply, but pursed his lips, looking pensive. In that moment, Kori thought he seemed very much like the doctor contemplating his patient's diagnosis.

Turning, she sat facing him, one leg tucked beneath her. "What are you thinking about, Dr. McDonald?" she asked with a smile.

"I'm thinking about how much I hate waiting!"

Kori leaned her head back and laughed out loud. "Now there's the Brent I remember!"

He smiled back at her and then looked at his watch. "But I shouldn't have to wait too much longer for my supper."

Kori's eyes widened. "I almost forgot about our meat loaf."

"Me too."

Getting up from the sofa, Brent took Kori's hand and helped her to her feet. He didn't release her, as she expected, but put his arms around her waist. Pulling her closer to him, he kissed her with a fervency that melted the years between them.

And it was a long while later before they remembered the meat loaf again.

thirteen

"So. You decided to come home, huh?"

At Clair's remark, Kori blushed; it was nearly two in the morning. "I fell asleep," she muttered, hanging up her coat. She didn't, however, say that she had fallen asleep in Brent's arms as they snuggled together on the couch and watched TV.

Clair, dressed in her nightgown and robe, had obviously gotten up for a glass of water. "Okay, let's hear it," she said in her sternest big-sister voice. "Where were you and who were you with? As if I need to even ask."

Kori laughed. "The three of us, Dana, you, and I, will make fine mothers."

"Don't change the subject," Clair retorted.

"Okay, I won't." Kori knew she didn't owe her sister an explanation, but she'd give her one anyway. While Dana, Clair, and Kori respected each other's privacy, they also expected responsibility. Right after Kori moved in, they made rules for themselves—no last-minute overnight guests, no staying out all night—and if one of those agreed upon rules were violated, the offender owed the others an explanation. They had all agreed that there was security in accountability. "I'm so late," Kori began, "because Brent talked me into making him dinner tonight. After we ate, I fell asleep on the couch while Brent watched TV. I woke up about an hour ago." Kori shrugged. "Brent said he didn't have the heart to wake me up earlier."

"All right," Clair said, a little smile tugging at the corners of her mouth, "you're off the hook. . .this time."

"Thanks, sis," Kori replied facetiously as she walked with Clair to the kitchen area.

"Kind of seems like you've made your decision about Brent."

Kori shrugged. "I'm no longer refusing to give our marriage another chance, if that's what you mean. But I still have to sort out my feelings. There are times, like tonight," she said candidly, "when I think I know what love is and that I'm still in love with Brent. But then there are other times when I remember how he left me and how he said he just didn't love me anymore. Then the questions start all over again. What is real love?" Kori sighed. "I know I need to sort out my feelings and make a decision soon."

Clair nodded.

"But here's the thing," Kori continued. "Feelings change. My deepest fear is that Brent will change his mind again."

"Kori, there are no guarantees in this life. Anyone could change his mind. Including Jared."

"No, not Jared."

"Yes, Jared," Clair said, pouring herself another glass of water. "A person can set his or her mind to anything, but then the circumstances change. I mean, Jared could get laid off of work or he could get a terminal illness, which could make him become a real homebody. Perhaps he'd see the value of a wife and kids. On the other hand, Jared might win the lottery and decide he doesn't want the burden of a family. He might decide to move to Key West and live like a recluse on a fishing boat the rest of his life."

Kori made a tsk-sound with her tongue. "Well, Brent could decide the same thing—as he so nonchalantly did once already!"

"Exactly my point. Circumstances change a person's feelings—Brent's, yours, mine, and Jared's."

"Okay, so how do I handle that?"

"You deal with your feelings as they change and expect that your 'significant other' will too. That's where commitment comes in. You trust each other enough to believe that you will both keep your promises despite the changes that are bound to come in life."

"But I need a guarantee," Kori contended. "I need something in this life that I can hang on to."

Clair drank her water and then set her glass in the sink. "Sorry, I can't help you there, kiddo. In my experience I've found that there are no guarantees in this life." She smiled and gave Kori a hug. "Good night."

"Good night."

Kori watched her sister walk through the living room and toward the bedrooms. She felt that abyss in her soul widen, but she couldn't figure out why. Kori had friends and coworkers who liked her, a sister who loved her, a roommate who cared almost as much as a sister, and two men who professed to be in love with her. Yet she felt like the loneliest person alive.

꙳

The next day, Kori was tired and distracted. She'd sit at her desk and try to do paperwork, but then she'd see Jared's picture and feel guilty. She wanted to blame Brent for tempting her even though he knew she was struggling; however, she was the one who had curled up beside him last night. She hadn't resisted his kisses—even the one he'd given her this morning after he drove her to work. It seemed that when she was with Brent, Kori forgot all about her commitment to Jared. What kind of a person was she anyway?

By the end of the day, Kori was irritable and confused, though she tried desperately not to show it. When she was short-tempered with a patient over the telephone, she felt even worse about herself.

"Kori, can I have a word with you?" Close to tears, she looked up from the route slips on her desk. Ryan stood at the doorway. "Let's go into my office."

Nodding solemnly, Kori followed Ryan down the corridor and into his office. He shut the door and she sat down.

"What's with you today? You're not yourself."

"That's for sure." Kori sighed as Ryan sat down behind his desk.

"What's going on?"

"Oh," she sighed, "it's this thing with Brent."

"Hmm. . ." He sat back in his chair. "You can't let personal matters interfere with your work, Kori."

"I know."

Ryan was momentarily thoughtful. "You want to fill me in on the situation? You don't have to, but maybe I can help."

Kori shrugged. "I'm torn between whether I should give my marriage another chance or start over with Jared."

Ryan grinned. "You've changed your tune since the last time we spoke about this."

"I know. Brent is very persuasive and I'm very confused." Kori sighed again, this time impatiently. "Which man do I give my heart to? Which one can guarantee me he won't break it?"

"Neither one, Kori," Ryan replied in soft concern. "Men and women alike are fallible human beings."

"Yes, I know. I guess it's just like Clair said: there are no guarantees in life."

"There is one."

"Oh?"

"Jesus Christ."

Kori rolled her eyes. "I should have known you were heading in that direction." She gave him a pointed look. "Don't preach at me, Ryan."

"Okay, but let me just say this: Jesus is the answer to your questions and the solution to your problems. Jesus is the one Man you can give your heart to, and He'll never break it because He loves you with a love that will never let you go."

Kori had gotten up from her chair and was heading toward the door when something clicked. She turned. "What did you say?"

"I said, Jesus is the answer to your questions—"

"No. I mean about the love that will never let me go."

Ryan looked a bit confused. "That's just what I said. Jesus Christ loves you with a love that will never let you go."

"How do you know that?"

Ryan smiled. "It's in the Bible. Christ promised it, and being the Son of God, He doesn't lie."

Kori stood frozen. On the one hand, she doubted that any form of religion would help her; on the other, something inside compelled her to hear more.

"Sit back down, Kori," Ryan said. "Our last patient cancelled and your paperwork can wait. We've worked together for the good part of two years now and I've been your friend as well as your physician."

Kori nodded, taking her seat once more. Ryan was a friend, that was true enough, and he had helped her overcome the depression that began after she moved to Wisconsin. Ryan had prescribed some antidepressants, which Kori took for only a short period of time. Meanwhile, Ryan monitored her closely, giving her friendly advice from time to time.

"As your friend," he continued, "I want to share the good news of salvation through Christ with you. As your physician—well, I don't want you to get so down that you fall into a depression again."

"I don't want that either."

Ryan smiled. "Will you let me tell you about the Savior then?"

"You've told me about Him a hundred times," Kori said despairingly.

"But will you listen this time?"

Kori considered the request as tears filled her eyes. Would she listen? Would it make a difference if she did? She needed something. . .

"Yes," she said at last, "I'll listen."

❧

When Kori left Ryan's office, she only felt more confused instead of consoled. Now there was a third Man tugging at her heart. A Man who was God, a Man named Jesus Christ. A Man who supposedly loved her enough to give His life for her.

Gathering her belongings in preparation to leave for the day, Kori tucked the little pamphlet that Ryan had given her into her purse. Over the years, Ryan had given Kori dozens of "tracts," as he called them, all of which she had deposited in her nightstand at home. She hadn't read them before, but maybe it was time to read them now.

Kori walked downstairs, got her coat, and then punched out for the day. Brent was waiting patiently in the lobby. Seeing her, he set down the magazine he'd been reading and smiled. Then he got a better look at Kori's face and frowned in concern.

"Are you all right? Bad day?"

"Yes and yes," Kori replied with a hint of a smile.

Brent walked beside her as they left the clinic, and Kori tried to ignore the curious stares from the receptionists. They knew she was engaged to Jared, and they were probably wondering who Brent was. Rumors were probably buzzing around the clinic like pesky flies at a summer barbecue. However, tonight Kori was too tired to care.

"Would you like some dinner?" Brent asked kindly. "I'll cook or we could eat out."

Kori only answered his question with one of her own. "Brent, who is Jesus Christ?"

He paused in the midst of opening up the passenger door of his truck. "Who is He?"

"Yes."

"He's the Son of God."

"I know that, but. . .who is He to you?"

"My Savior."

"Yes, but—"

Brent chuckled. "Get in the truck and we'll talk on the way home. It's freezing out here and this conversation could take a while."

Kori climbed in and waited until Brent was seated and had started the engine. "Ryan and I were talking about Jesus Christ this afternoon."

"Oh, yeah?" Brent sounded pleased.

"Ryan told me that I need to give my heart to Jesus—but how can I do that if I don't know who He is?"

"Hmm. . .good question. Let me think about it for a minute."

Kori leaned back against the seat and closed her eyes while Brent pondered the inquiry.

"To me," he said at last, "Jesus Christ is like a brother with whom I am very close. He's also my best friend and, like the Bible says, He is the Great Physician, so in that way—in every way—Jesus Christ is my mentor. I can go to Christ with all my problems and leave them with Him, knowing He has the power to take care of them and me because He is God." Brent glanced at Kori. "And, being God, He expects me not to sin, though He will forgive me when I do and when I ask Him to forgive me. Christ also expects me to live up to the standards He set in the Holy Bible. He died on the cross for my sins, rose again from the dead, and now we have a relationship." Brent paused. "I hope that's not too pat of an answer, but it's the truth as I understand it."

Kori nodded, and wondered who Jesus Christ was to her. She didn't think she needed a brother or a "Great Physician." She didn't even need another friend. What she needed was a love that would never let her go. But how could she find that in Jesus Christ?

She was so deep in thought that she didn't even notice where Brent was taking her until he stopped and shut off the engine. They were in the parking lot of a Greek restaurant.

"Would you like to eat here?"

Kori thought it over and then shook her head. "No, I need to go home, Brent. I'm tired."

He nodded and restarted the engine.

"Thanks anyway, though."

"You bet."

By the time they arrived at her apartment, Kori decided that she at least owed Brent some supper for driving her to and from work. In just a few days she'd have her own new car and her independence back again.

"Want to come in?" she asked after Brent parked. "I'll

make you something to eat."

"Thanks, Kori. I'll take you up on the offer."

They walked into the apartment complex and then up to Kori's apartment. Clair and Dana still weren't home and the place was dark. While Brent waited in the small hallway, Kori made her way into the living room and turned on a lamp. Then she returned and hung up their coats.

"Come on in and sit down, Brent," she said. "I'll start supper. How about a gourmet dish—like macaroni and cheese?"

Brent laughed. "That sounds great, Kori."

"Dana will have a fit when she finds out I made this," Kori told him, taking the box out of the cupboard. "Dana hates prepackaged food."

"Well, I'm not that way. In fact," Brent added, a mischievous gleam in his eyes, "why don't I make the macaroni and cheese while you slip into something more comfortable?"

"Oh, quiet!" Kori told him on a sarcastic note, while Brent laughed, sounding thoroughly amused by his own humor. Then even Kori had to chuckle.

"Oh, well," Brent said at last, "you can't blame a guy for trying."

Kori rolled her eyes and pulled out a saucepan.

"You know," Brent said, "I think you'd enjoy meeting Mark and Juli."

Something pulled at Kori's insides at the mention of Brent's friends. She hoped Brent wasn't trying to mimic Mark and Julia's reunion.

She set the pan of water on the stove and turned on the burner. "When did you want to reconcile with me, Brent?" she asked calculatingly.

"What do you mean?"

"When was it? A month after you found out we were still married? Two months? When?"

Brent thought it over. "I think it was probably the very night Tom Sandersfeld told me the divorce never went through. In fact, a couple days after my dad and I met with Tom, I called him and told him to put the divorce papers on hold until I got back to him. I told him I had a lot of thinking to do.

"You see, after you moved here to Wisconsin, Kori, I had already begun to regret our separation. I had learned that being a bachelor wasn't so great. It was lonely. The dating scene was pathetic and I didn't want any part of it. And my hot red sports car certainly didn't snuggle up next to me at night."

Brent grinned meaningfully and Kori blushed. She certainly *had* snuggled up next to him last night!

Kori cleared her throat. "And when did you talk to Mark Henley and find out about him and Juli?"

"Let's see. . .must have been in September." Brent gave her a smile. "I told Mark I'd stand up in his wedding and then I stewed some more over what to do about you and me. Finally I concluded that it was just too coincidental that Mark was getting married here in Wisconsin and you lived in Wisconsin. So I prayed about it and now I really believe that it's God's will for our marriage to be a success. When I told Mark that I was taking some time off to get my wife back, he really encouraged me."

"So you talked to God before Mark Henley?"

Brent nodded and then frowned curiously. "Why do you ask, Kori?"

She shrugged. "I guess I'm glad you talked to God first."

A slow smile spread across Brent's darkly handsome face but he didn't say anymore. Instead, he picked up one of Dana's banking magazines, sat down on the sofa, and leafed through it. In the kitchen, Kori added the macaroni to the boiling water and decided that there was something comforting about a man who talked to God. Like Ryan Carlson.

Then she thought about Ryan and Stacie. Kori envied their relationship, the closeness they seemed to share. Could she and Brent experience that?

Maybe our marriage does deserve another chance, she mused. *Maybe my second time around should be with Brent. Perhaps we could get it right this time. . .*

fourteen

Kori smoothed on some lipstick and then pressed her lips together.

"Where you going?" Dana wanted to know as she entered the bathroom and grabbed her hairbrush. "Have a hot date?" She laughed.

Kori was chuckling, too. "Yeah, my hot date is taking me to church."

"To church?"

Clair had been walking by the bathroom, and she paused outside the door. "Did I hear you say you're going to church, Korah Mae?"

"Yep. You heard right." Both Dana and Clair were now watching Kori expectantly. "Before I agree to give Brent and our marriage a second chance," she explained, "I decided I'd better find out if this born-again Christian stuff is something I can live with."

Clair leaned against the doorway. "Don't you think that it's just another passing fad with Brent?"

Kori bit her lower lip and momentarily contemplated the question. "You know," she said at last, "I guess I'm hoping it's not. Since Brent got religious, he's different. . .and I like the difference. If his faith lasts, so will our marriage. I'm sure of it."

"But there's no guarantee it will last," Clair said. "That shouldn't be a basis for your decision."

"True. But on the other hand, if Brent's religion is too weird, then I can't live with that, either. And that's why I'm going to church tonight."

Clair nodded, looking disinterested. "Well, have fun," she said, walking away.

"You know, I used to go to church," Dana confided. "When

121

I was a teenager. I was part of a youth group. But then I guess I drifted away." She paused. "But I still believe in God and I pray."

"I don't have much church experience," Kori admitted. "My parents took Clair and me to church for weddings, funerals, sometimes at Christmas, but that's it."

Dana got a faraway look in her eyes. "Wow, I haven't been to church in a long time. Seems like forever."

"You're welcome to come with me tonight."

"Yeah?" She thought it over. "Maybe I will."

"Better hurry and decide. I have to leave in five minutes. Clair said I could use her car tonight."

"Well, we can take mine." Dana smiled broadly. "I'll go change my clothes."

Kori watched as Dana bounded into her bedroom and whipped open her closet door. Smiling after her, Kori left the bathroom and walked into the living room.

"You know," Clair said, looking pensive, "maybe I should go with you. I mean, tomorrow is Thanksgiving Day and I have to meet Zach's entire family. I suppose a prayer or two wouldn't hurt, huh?"

Kori shrugged. "The more the merrier."

Minutes later, the three friends were climbing into Clair's car, since it was the larger of the two. Kori assumed the role of navigator, and within twenty minutes, they were pulling into the church parking lot.

Brent met them at the door and ushered them into the spacious lobby of the large church. "All three of you came. What a surprise."

"Yeah, well, Dana and I decided that we could probably use a little church, too," Clair explained.

Brent smiled warmly. "Great. Let's hang up your coats and go get a seat."

They followed Brent to the other side of the lobby where he solicitously hung up each lady's wrap. Then they followed him into the auditorium.

"I just love these modern-looking churches," Dana remarked as they sat down in the padded pew. Brent was on the end, Kori beside him, and then Dana and Clair next to her. "They're not so imposing, you know?"

Kori agreed, deciding that she liked the music, too. It was lively, happy. Someone played the piano while another played the organ.

Then the service began and the congregation sang a couple of hymns. After that the youth group sang.

"Oh, this reminds me of my old youth group," Dana said nostalgically.

An offering was taken then, followed by the pastor's sermon. He spoke on the power of the Holy Spirit in a true believer's life. Kori wasn't exactly sure what the pastor was talking about, though she'd heard of the Trinity: Father, Son, Holy Spirit. Ryan had explained it and, as the pastor kept talking, certain things began to make sense to Kori. So far, nothing was too weird for her.

Once the pastor finished his sermon, he asked for prayer requests. One by one church members stood and revealed problems in their lives that required prayer. Some stood and gave "a praise." They told of how God had directed them, provided for them, and answered their prayers. It was all a little much for Kori to fathom. Wasn't God too busy to be bothered which such trivial things as a new job or a new house? Couldn't these people just make their own decisions? Perhaps they were weak-minded.

Then Kori spotted Ryan sitting several pews ahead of her. Beside him sat Stacie Rollins. Kori watched as she leaned over and whispered something to Ryan. He nodded in reply.

So much for my theory, she mused. *Ryan isn't weak-minded and, from what I remember, Stacie isn't either.*

Kori looked at Brent who was writing down a prayer request on a sheet of paper. Her weak-minded theory might apply to him, but only in the way that the Brent she once knew went from one cause to the next. Could she live with this one?

His religion seemed harmless enough. In fact, it seemed pro-marriage, pro-family—the very things Kori desired.

Suddenly Brent looked up at her and smiled. She smiled back and it was then that Kori realized she'd rather go to church with Brent than go to a bar or bowling alley with Jared.

The service ended and before she knew it, a small group had congregated around them, Ryan and Stacie included.

"Kori, your coming to the worship service tonight is answered prayer for me," Ryan told her, grinning broadly.

"Good," she replied facetiously. "Maybe now you won't bug me about visiting any more."

He laughed.

Stacie was smiling. "I used to think the same thing when Julia here would invite me out to hear the gospel. It sounded so. . .boring."

"I only asked you a few times," replied the lovely lady with thick, auburn hair. "And the very first time you agreed to come."

"I haven't been sorry, either," Stacie said.

A tall man with blond hair, blue eyes, and broad shoulders chuckled. He stuck his right hand out to Kori. "Nice to see you again."

She recognized him then. "Mark Henley." She shook his hand. "Nice to see you, too."

"Who would have ever thought we'd all meet up again in Wisconsin?" Mark said, giving Brent a friendly slap on the back. "Huh, California boy?"

Brent just grinned in reply. Then he introduced the group to Clair and Dana.

"The four of us are going out for pizza," Julia said, looking at Kori. "Would all of you like to join us?"

"Oh, that sounds fun!" Dana piped in. She looked at Mark. "How's the singles' group in this church. . .not that I'm interested or anything?"

Everyone burst out in laughter and Clair gave Dana a playful shove.

Mark glanced at Julia. "How's the singles' group here?" He turned back and explained, "I'm really just a visitor. I'm a consultant and travel all over the country. But I've been in Wisconsin for almost six months now. However, Julia has been a member of this church for years. So has Ryan."

"Actually, the singles' group could use new blood," she replied with a smile. "Especially since Ryan and Stacie are an 'item.'"

"Well, I'll keep that in mind," Dana said, looking sheepish.

Clair rolled her eyes and Kori laughed.

"Let's go eat," Ryan suggested. "I'm starved."

🔊

Kori put her key in the lock and opened the apartment door. Clair and Dana followed her in.

"Oh, that was fun!" Dana exclaimed, flouncing on the sofa. "I'm stuffed."

"Me too," Clair said, taking a seat in the armchair.

Kori sat in other. "I did more talking than eating tonight. Imagine that."

Clair grinned. "You and Juli were having quite the intense conversation."

Kori nodded. "She and Mark went through something like Brent and I are experiencing, only there was a child involved. Julia and Mark have a son named Jesse."

"No kidding?" Dana sat up, looking interested. "But they're not married, so. . .what happened?"

"It happened in high school," Kori explained. "Mark and Julia were young and in love and they weren't Christians. They were planning to get married after Julia graduated, but Mark got cold feet. . .on the day of the wedding. A couple of months later, Juli realized she was pregnant, but Mark had moved out of state by then."

"You know, I saw a movie like that once. What was the name of it again. . .?"

Clair shot a pillow at her. "Will you quit with your movies already? You watch too much TV."

In reply, Dana shot the pillow back at Clair. She looked at Kori then. "So Mark and Julia just got reunited, huh?"

"Yes. Julia said she burned her bridges when she left the small town she grew up in. Mark had been looking for her, but couldn't find her. Then, finally, he met up with her at work. He was hired as a consultant and Julia was some manager or something. They're both Christians now and they've worked things out between them. And they're getting married next month!"

"What a sweet story," Dana cooed.

"Is that for real, Kori?"

She nodded. "I have no reason to believe Julia would lie."

"I know. . .but, well, it sounds so pat. Real life isn't like that. Love and forgiveness and happily-ever-after."

"It is if you want it to be," Dana replied.

Kori agreed. "And God has a big part of it. I mean, that's what Julia kept saying."

"Do you believe that, Kori?" Clair wanted to know.

She thought it over. "You know," she replied at last. "I think I'm beginning to." The admission surprised even Kori.

"So you're going to give Brent another chance?" Dana asked.

"I'm certainly leaning that way."

"I think you two belong together," Clair stated.

"I'm starting to agree," Dana added. "But I feel sorry for Jared."

Kori sighed. "Yes, and I don't want to hurt him. I have to talk to him after he gets home from deer hunting." She stood. "Well, I'd better turn in. I've got a busy day tomorrow." She smiled, looking forward to her newly made Thanksgiving Day plans. "Brent is picking me up for something called a 'praise service' and then we're going to Julia's aunt's for dinner. Julia extended the invitation tonight."

"What about that Deer Hunter Widows' Ball you're supposed to attend tomorrow night?" Dana asked.

Kori shrugged. "I won't be going. I don't have a car and

Brent certainly won't drive me to a tavern. I'm sure he considers it a modern-day den of iniquity, so I'm not even going to ask him for the favor."

Clair chuckled. "Brent has been against drinking alcoholic beverages for a long time. That's nothing new. Remember the time we were at Mom and Dad's for dinner and he gave us a big lecture about the effects of alcohol on the brain? He'd seen some study in one of his medical classes. And there we were sitting around the table, sipping red wine. . . none of us could even finish it once Brent had his say."

"I remember," Kori said, laughing at the memory. "Well, in any case," she continued, "I'm sure I won't even be missed tomorrow night. Sounds like there's going to be a large crowd. I heard an ad for the party on a local radio station yesterday morning." She turned to leave. "Guess I'll trot off to bed. G'night, ladies."

Clair stood. "I'm going to bed, too. Good night, ladies," she mimicked.

"Hey, isn't that a song?" Dana cried. Then she began to sing. "Good night, ladies. Good night, ladies. Good night, ladies. . ."

Chuckling at her roommate, Kori proceeded down the hallway to her bedroom. She closed the door behind her and undressed for bed. Slipping her nightgown over her head, her ring caught on the seam of the sleeve and, disengaging it, she peered at the diamond on her left hand. Her conscience pricked her. She felt like a hypocrite.

Suddenly Kori knew she was standing on one of life's many bridges. She either had to go one way or another. Cross over to a marital relationship with Jared, or go back to Brent.

A long moment passed. Then another. Finally, Kori slowly slipped the ring off her finger.

fifteen

Thanksgiving dawned, another frosty November day. Gazing out her apartment window, Kori thought about the house Brent had purchased in California. She remembered its redecorating needs and decided she'd like to be the one to do them. Besides, she missed California. These Wisconsin winters could be so long.

Then she thought about Jared. Kori hated the thought of breaking his heart. If only there were some other way. . .

Glancing at her wristwatch, Kori realized that Brent would be waiting for her outside in just a few minutes. She grabbed her purse and coat, called a good-bye to Clair and Dana who were just rolling out of bed, and walked down to the lobby. She immediately spotted Brent's forest-green 4 X 4. Amazingly, he was early!

"Hi," he said as she climbed into the truck, "you look nice."

Holding her coat, Kori gave him a self-conscious smile. "I wasn't sure what to wear, so I settled for this skirt and sweater." She shrugged.

"You look great," Brent replied as he pulled away from the curb.

"Not overdressed or too casual?"

"I think you're dressed just right," Brent said with an amused chuckle.

Kori lifted a brow. "And I think you're impressed much too easily these days."

"Oh?" A little grin played on his lips.

Then she added, "But I like it."

Brent laughed heartily. "Are you telling me that I was hard to impress during the course of our marriage?"

Kori smiled gently. "No, I'm not, because you really weren't

128

hard to impress or please, Brent. I'm just saying. . . well, I like the change in you."

He glanced over at her, a tender expression on his face.

Some twenty minutes later, Brent pulled into the church parking lot. "The service this morning," he explained as they walked toward the building, "is exclusively music and testimonies of praise."

Kori nodded. "Yes, that's what Julia told me last night."

They entered the rapidly filling auditorium and found a seat beside Ryan and Stacie. Brent was on the end, sitting to Kori's left.

Ryan leaned forward, looking at her. "Glad to see you, Kori—again!"

She had to laugh. For all the many times Ryan had asked her to visit his church, he probably never thought it would happen twice in the same week.

The Thanksgiving Day service began and Kori was impressed with the instrumental solos as well as the congregational singing. She didn't know any of the "hymns of praise," as the music director called them; however, she caught on quickly. The testimonies were interspersed throughout the service, and Kori found herself curious once more over the dependence these people had on their God. They seemed to count on Him to solve their every problem and supply their every need. Weak-minded. . .?

Then Kori thought about her own situation—the one with Jared. She'd love to turn the responsibility of breaking her engagement over to an all-controlling God who loved her and wanted to protect her. But who was He and how did one go about getting God to do such marvelous things?

Brent suddenly reached out and took Kori's hand. Their fingers entwined and Kori sensed that he'd taken note of her bare ring finger. She stole a glance at him and nearly laughed out loud at Brent's astonished expression. He only tightened his hold on her hand and a contented warmth spread throughout her being.

Shortly thereafter, the service ended and Kori followed Brent out of the auditorium. In the spacious, well-decorated vestibule, they met up with Julia and Mark. An older couple stood beside them.

"Kori and Brent," Julia began, "I'd like you to meet Barb and Glen French. They're like my second parents."

The introductions were made and then Barb looked at her watch. "Oh, mercy!" she exclaimed. "The turkey will be done in two hours, and I still have mashed potatoes to make and a table to set."

"Don't worry, we'll help," Julia assured the older woman.

Kori heartily concurred.

"Well, then," Barb replied, "let's go!"

Outside in the parking lot, Brent unlocked the truck's passenger door. Before opening it, however, he paused and the November wind tousled his thick, sable hair. "You took off your engagement ring."

Kori just nodded, looking back into his probing gaze.

"What does that mean?"

She took a deep breath. "It means I felt like a hypocrite wearing it."

"That's all?"

Brent looked crestfallen and the expression on his face tugged at Kori's heartstrings. It was then she knew that if she hadn't made up her mind before, she had now.

"I can hardly wear Jared's engagement ring," she said with an intent look into Brent's dark gaze, "when I want to give our marriage another chance."

Brent swooped her up into his arms before the last word had even passed her lips. He swung her around in a full circle and several passing church members gazed at them curiously.

"Good grief, Brent!" she chided when he finally set her down. "What will people think?"

"Who cares? I'm the happiest man alive right now!" With a lopsided grin, he opened the truck's door and helped Kori climb inside.

The Frenches' home was located on the north side of Menomonee Falls, so Brent had to pass his apartment to get there. "Do you mind if I make a quick stop?" he asked, pulling into the complex's parking lot.

"Not at all. Did you forget something?"

"Sort of." Brent opened the door and climbed out of the truck. "Why don't you come on inside with me?"

"But—"

Brent closed his door behind him, cutting off her reply. *Impetuous,* she thought. *Now there's a word that describes my Brent. My Brent. . .*Kori's heart repeated those words. *Can this really be happening?* she had to wonder. *Brent and I back together again?* She sighed and then realized, *If he's the "happiest man alive" right now, then I'm the happiest woman!*

She opened the door and he was right there waiting for her to exit the truck. He grabbed her hand and led her toward the front door of the apartment.

"The Frenches are waiting," Kori gently reminded him as Brent pulled out his keys. "And Barb wanted some help with—"

"This won't take long."

Brent let her into the apartment, and as Kori entered the living room, he rushed down the hallway toward the bedrooms. Shaking her head at him, Kori looked around. The boxes Brent had brought from California still lay in the corner. She was glad now that he hadn't thrown them away as she'd requested; however, she still thought the majority of their contents were useless junk.

Her gaze traveled from the boxes to the neatly stacked piles beside them. Kori's needlework was in one and their photo albums were in another. Then Kori spotted the musical carousel. Relief washed over her; Brent hadn't discarded it after all! Walking over to where it sat on the coffee table, Kori lifted it gently, cradling it in her hands.

Brent entered the room then, wearing a broad smile and looking like the cat that swallowed the canary.

Kori lifted a brow. "What are you up to?"

He laughed and, closing the distance between them, he took the music box. After replacing it on the coffee table, Brent looked back at her and smiled even more broadly. "Close your eyes and hold out your hand."

Kori gave him an incredulous-sounding laugh. "No way, Brent. Last time you told me to do that, you stuck something in my hand from your biology lab."

He hooted. "Oh, yeah, I had forgotten about that. Funny!"

"No, it was gross!"

"Well, this surprise isn't gross at all," Brent promised between chortles. "Really, Kori. Now, close your eyes."

Grudgingly, she obeyed. With her hand outstretched, she felt Brent set something small and soft on her palm.

"It doesn't feel slimy."

Brent chuckled again. "It's not. Okay, open your eyes."

She did and, there in her hand was a black velvet-covered box.

"Open it up," Brent encouraged her.

Kori lifted the lid, already suspecting its contents. However, she breathed an "Oh, Brent!" upon seeing the sparkling diamond wedding band inside.

"I bought it a few days ago," he told her. "It was going to be a bribe. You know, the guy with the best diamond ring wins."

Kori rolled her eyes at the facetious statement.

"Here, let's see if it fits." Brent took the ring out of its satin cradle and slipped it onto Kori's finger. "It's a bit big, but we can take it back and get it sized." He searched her face. "Do you like it?"

"Yes. It's beautiful," Kori murmured, staring at the marquis diamond, set onto a gold band that shimmered from her finger. On either side of the stone were two smaller diamonds. Looking back at Brent, she smiled and teasingly said, "I guess you win."

Brent narrowed his dark gaze. "About time."

Then he stepped forward, drew Kori into his arms, and kissed her with all the passion of a husband.

*

"We were beginning to think you two got lost," Mark said, opening the front door of the Frenches' home. Smiling, he welcomed Kori and Brent inside. "Here, let me take your coats."

"I had to make a stop at my place," Brent explained.

"Well, I'm glad you finally made it."

They followed Mark into the living room where a fire burned in the fireplace.

"Hi, Kori," Julia said, waving to her from where she sat on the couch.

Kori returned Julia's greeting and then said hello to Stacie and Ryan. Lastly, she was introduced to Mark and Julia's eleven-year-old son Jesse.

"So, what took you so long?" Ryan asked from the swivel-rocker in which he sat.

Kori felt a silly blush warm her cheeks as Brent took her left hand and held it up, ring side out. "Kori has agreed to give our marriage another chance," he announced.

Congratulatory cheers rang throughout the living room, adding to Kori's embarrassment. However, she couldn't deny the happiness in her heart as she and Brent sat down on the couch.

Julia, sitting on the other side of her, took hold of Kori's left hand. "I've got to have a better look here." She scrutinized the wedding band and then looked over at Brent. "Beautiful ring. You did a nice job in choosing it."

"Thanks," Brent replied, looking somewhat embarrassed.

Julia then had to show off her engagement ring to Kori and the conversation turned to the upcoming wedding, set to take place next month.

Minutes later, Barb and Glen entered the room and sat down. "We have a good half hour till dinner," Barb announced. "We can all just sit and relax and enjoy each other's company. Everything is done. We're just waiting on the old bird."

Kori smiled at the older woman just as Julia stood and began taking orders for coffee, tea, or punch.

"I'll help you," Kori insisted, gathering a few glasses from outstretched hands. Then she followed Julia into the kitchen.

"I'm so happy for you and Brent," Julia stated once she and Kori were alone.

"Thank you," Kori replied, setting down the glasses. "I'm happy for us, too."

Julia smiled as she juggled several cups and saucers. "Oh, dear, looks like I'll have to make another pot of coffee," she said, glancing at the empty pot. She looked back at Kori. "You don't have to wait. You're free to join the others if you'd like. Barb's coffeemaker is rather slow."

"I'll wait, if you don't mind." Kori paused. "I'd like to ask you a couple of questions."

"Sure."

Kori waited until Julia had prepared the coffee in the automatic maker.

"Why don't we sit over at the kitchen table," Julia suggested. "What's on your mind?"

"Well. . ." Kori really didn't know where to begin; however, she sensed a kindred spirit in Julia and felt that she could open up to her. "I have some. . .spiritual questions."

"All right. I'll try to answer them."

Kori began slowly. "I understand that in order to be born again, I have to give Jesus my heart. . .but I don't know who He is or how I go about giving my heart to Him—or even what that means, to tell you the truth."

"Hmm. . ." Julia pensively chewed her lower lip. "I don't know where to begin."

"Will you start by telling me who Jesus Christ is to you?"

"Sure. He's my God, my Savior, the Lover of my soul, and the best, most dearest Friend I have."

"Even better than Mark?" Kori asked incredulously.

"Yep. You see, Jesus Christ is the only One who doesn't change. He's the same—yesterday, today, and forever. People change, but God doesn't."

Kori was very interested now. Perhaps Jesus Christ was

that "guarantee" she'd been searching for.

"Mark could change, so I can't build my life around him, even though I know he is the one God would have for me to marry. And Mark has God's Holy Spirit living in his heart, just as I do, so we've got a solid foundation upon which to build our marital relationship."

"And if Mark would ever leave you, or say he didn't love you any more. . .?"

Julia gave Kori an empathetic look. "It's a scary thought, isn't it? If Mark left me, it would hurt beyond what words could tell." She paused, looking thoughtful. "But, if that happened, I'd always have Jesus. Only He is my anchor, not a man. Not Mark, though I love Mark very much." Julia smiled. "Am I making sense?"

Slowly, Kori nodded. "I think I know what you're talking about, because I built my whole world around Brent once."

"Only Jesus," Julia said. "A person can only build a life or a relationship around Him."

"And He is the. . .the Lover of my soul."

Julia nodded. "He loved you so much, Kori, He gave His life for you."

"For the world," Kori restated, questioningly.

"No," Julia said, "for *you*, Kori. If you were the only person on earth, Jesus would have still gone to the cross. *For you.*"

Kori was momentarily thoughtful. "That's an awesome idea, Julia," she said at last. "Jesus Christ loving me so much that He gave His life. . .for me."

"For you."

"But for you, too."

Julia nodded. "Yes. However, you've got to take this matter of salvation very personally, Kori, because it's strictly between you and Jesus. And when you accept Him as your personal Savior, He has your heart. That's when it happens."

Kori nodded, beginning to understand. "But what if Brent decides he doesn't want to be a born-again Christian any more? What if this is just another passing fad with him?"

Julia was momentarily thoughtful. "Well, Brent could certainly let go of Christ, but Christ won't ever let go of him. The Holy Spirit would continue to work on Brent's heart." Julia leaned over in a conspiratorial way. "I think you're going to find that the most wonderful thing about having a Christian husband, Kori, is that if he gets out of line, God will discipline him. Brent will get a spiritual spanking from his Heavenly Father—and that's a promise from the Bible."

"A guarantee."

Julia nodded. "I've gotten plenty of spiritual spankings, Kori," she added, "and they hurt. But I'm so glad God loves me enough to show me when I'm wrong and out of His perfect will. Then, once I understand that I was wrong, I simply ask for God's forgiveness and my relationship with Him is restored."

"Well, thanks, Julia. I really appreciate you taking this time with me."

"My pleasure. And it looks like our coffee is ready, too."

Julia got up from the table and poured the steaming brew into the coffee cups while Kori filled the waiting glasses with punch. She was pensive all the while. Then, as she followed Julia back into the living room, Kori said a silent prayer: *Jesus, I want to accept You as my Savior, my Friend. . .the Lover of my soul. I don't really know what I'm doing, since I never prayed like this before, but I want to give You my heart because I want. . .no, I need Your guarantee.*

Then, as she handed back punch glasses and took her place beside Brent, Kori sensed she'd somehow obtained the very thing she'd asked for.

sixteen

"Kori, I think you're a Christian now," Brent told her later. It was nearing midnight as they sat in Brent's truck in front of Kori's apartment complex. She had just finished telling him about her conversation with Julia that afternoon and now, with the dome light on and his Bible open, Brent was trying to help Kori figure out what exactly occurred afterward.

"See," he said, pointing to the Scriptures, "this is what the Bible calls it. . .being saved." Then he read Romans 10:13 (KJV): " 'For whosoever shall call upon the name of the Lord shall be saved.' " He looked back at Kori. "Is that what you did? You called upon the Lord?"

"I think so."

Brent smiled and quizzed her further. "Do you believe God the Father raised God the Son from the dead. . .just like it says here in verse nine?"

"Well, if the Bible says so, then I believe it." Kori tapped her forefinger on the open Book. "This is my guarantee. Right?"

"God's Word, your guarantee?" Brent shrugged. "Sure, you could say that. I'm no theologian, Kori, and only God knows the heart, but it sounds to me like you got saved."

"I think I did," she replied, still trying to fully understand what had happened today.

Brent smiled warmly. "This truly has been a day of thanksgiving, hasn't it?"

"Yes, it has." Kori sighed happily. "I never thought this day would come. . .the two of us back together again. Reunited."

"Which brings me to another point I'd like to make." Brent closed his Bible, setting it down gingerly. "You're my wife, Kori, and I refuse to continue dropping you off at separate living quarters."

137

"I know," she replied. "I've been thinking about that tonight, too."

"And?"

"And. . .I suppose I could pack up what I have and move in with you. I really don't have any big furniture to speak of. Before I moved in, Clair and Dana used my room as a guest bedroom."

"Good. I was hoping you'd say that. And you don't mind leaving Wisconsin come January?"

"Are you kidding?" Kori laughed. "January is the best time to leave Wisconsin!"

Brent grinned at the tart reply. "What about your career?"

She shrugged. "There are plenty of jobs in California."

"You don't have to go back to work, Kori. I mean that."

"Good," she retorted. "Maybe I won't."

They shared a laugh.

"Really, Brent," she continued, "some of these things we'll just have to decide later—like whether or not I go to work after we move back to California." Kori sighed, a weighty issue still pressing upon her. "Right now I have to concentrate on breaking off my engagement to Jared—without breaking his heart."

"Maybe we can talk to him together," Brent suggested. "I don't like the idea of you seeing him alone, and if I'm there, maybe emotions won't fly as high as if it were just the two of you. In the last two years I've had to handle some crisis situations concerning my patients and their families and I think, by God's grace, I've handled them well."

"I'm sure you have, Brent," Kori replied. She had all the confidence in the world in him. Brent, no doubt, was a wonderful emergency physician. Caring, compassionate. . .and she was touched by his desire to help her out of this situation with Jared. "Let me think about it," she said at last. "I don't know what the best way is—or if there even is a 'best way.' "

"Listen," Brent said in a more serious tone, "it's admirable that you want to spare the guy any heartache, but it may not happen that way."

"I know."

He smiled gently. "The good news is we've both got the Lord now. If we ask Him, He'll see us through this."

"Oh, yes," Kori replied, smiling right back. "Dependence on God—like those testimonies this morning."

"That's right. . .now, give me a kiss good-bye," Brent told her, his arm circling her shoulders, his hand coming to rest on the back of her neck. "Tomorrow night, I won't be dropping you off." Then, after a lingering kiss, he let her go.

"Oh, and don't forget," he added, once Kori was out of the truck, "we can pick up your new car tomorrow."

She smiled. "Let's pick it up right after you help me move."

"It's a date." A tender expression crossed his face. "I love you so much, Kori."

"I love you, too." The words came so easily and were so heartfelt that Kori knew she meant them. And in that moment, she also realized she knew what love was—it was there all along. "I guess that was the problem between Jared and me," she mused aloud. "I wanted so badly to fall in love with him, but I couldn't because, all this time, I've been in love with you. I don't think I ever stopped loving you, Brent."

His dark eyes shone with adoration. "I know that I never stopped loving you." Then he grinned suggestively. "Sure you don't want to come home with me right now?"

Kori had to think about that one. She longed for Brent the way any wife longed for her husband; but she had made a pact with her roommates. Besides, she felt she needed to end one chapter in her life—the one with Jared—before beginning another with Brent.

"Tomorrow," she said on a decisive note. "I promise."

"Until tomorrow then," Brent replied, his gaze refusing to release hers.

Impulsively, Kori climbed back into the truck and gave Brent one more kiss. He chuckled in surprise and even Kori had to laugh softly as she tore herself away from him and then made her way up to the apartment building. She felt so lighthearted and happy, and so very much in love.

Kori reached the front door, and fishing in her purse, she pulled out her keys. She never saw the other truck in the parking lot, idling in the darkness.

❧

"Jared was here about a half hour ago," Dana announced as Kori entered their apartment.

"Jared?" Kori frowned. "He's supposed to be deer hunting."

"Yeah, well, he came back early. He said all the guys had planned to crash the ladies' party tonight—the one you were supposed to attend. Then when you didn't show up, he tried to call, but of course no one was here to answer the phone. Finally, he came over. I had just gotten home."

"What did you tell him?"

"Just that your car broke down so you didn't have a ride to the tavern and that you had decided to spend Thanksgiving Day with some new friends you'd met at church."

Kori hung up her coat. "How did Jared respond?"

"Okay, I guess. I know he understood about your car breaking down."

Kori nodded and met Dana in the living room. "Just so you know, Brent and I are officially back together," she said, holding out her left hand and showing off her ring.

Dana gasped. "That's the most gorgeous wedding band I've ever laid eyes on! I can see why you took him back."

"Oh, quiet!"

They laughed together and then Dana gave Kori a sisterly hug.

"I'm so happy for you," her friend said sincerely. "You and Brent. . .oh! I had a feeling you two belonged together ever since that first day when I saw him kiss you here in the living room." She paused, her delighted expression changing to one of concern. "But now you've got to break the news to Jared, huh?"

Again, Kori nodded. "It's going to be hard, too, because I

eally don't want to hurt him." She looked at the wedding band on her finger and uneasiness rose up inside her.

≈

The next morning at breakfast, Kori divulged her plans to her roommates. She was moving in with Brent this weekend and, come January, the two of them would move back to California. Since all three ladies had taken the day off from work, they lingered around the dining room table, sipping coffee and discussing Kori's departure.

"I'll sure miss you, Kori," Dana told her, looking sad.

"You'll just have to come and visit me in California. Brent bought a huge house! I can't wait for you to see it."

Dana's blue eyes sparkled with the notion. "Come February, I just might take you up on that offer."

"I hope you do."

Clair sipped her coffee. "It only makes sense that you and Brent get back together. A match made in heaven if I ever saw one!"

Kori chuckled. Her sister had said that very same thing on the day she married Brent.

"I was so angry and disappointed," Clair continued, "when I found out he'd left you. I wanted to wring Brent's neck." She took another sip of coffee. "But I guess he's redeemed himself satisfactorily."

"I'm sure he'll be glad you approve," Kori quipped.

Light laughter flitted around the table.

"And, speaking of approval, I have to call Mom and Dad and let them know." Kori stood, feeling amazed at the miraculous turn of events in these past weeks. Walking over to the phone, she picked it up and dialed her parents' home in Idaho.

Kori suspected that when Brent left her two and a half years ago, her father would have gladly joined Clair in "wringing his neck." However, her mother had been as heartbroken as Kori, saying she felt like she'd lost her only son. Then, when she'd informed her parents of her relationship with Jared, neither had seemed all that thrilled, though they acted happy for her, perhaps because she was their daughter and because Kori had wanted so badly to be in love and married again. And, though her parents had readily agreed to meet Jared over the Christmas holiday, Kori surmised they'd be more than pleased to hear of her reunion with Brent.

She wasn't wrong, either. Her mother squealed with joy and then made such a fuss that Kori had to hold the portable phone away from her ear. Clair even heard the excitement emanating from their mother clear across the room.

Shaking her head and rolling her eyes, Clair said, "Korah Mae, you'll be the talk of the bridge club tonight."

"Probably the bowling league, too," she replied, with a hand over the mouthpiece of the telephone. Her father was now on the line.

They talked, Kori repeating her good news, her father's reaction a subdued replica of his wife's. Then finally she gave the telephone over to Clair.

"Good morning, Dad. . .yes, it is exciting. Yes, Brent finally came to his senses." Kori watched as her older sister frowned. "What do you mean, when am I getting married? Soon, Dad. Zach and I are just making sure. No, no. . .he hasn't proposed yet. . ."

Chuckling softly at the parental interrogation Clair was forced to undergo, Kori left the living room and began packing her things. Amazingly, she discovered she'd accumulated more than she thought. Then, with Dana's help, she dug up a couple of cardboard boxes, but she'd need to find several more to get the job done.

At noon, the doorbell chimed. Kori assumed Brent had arrived to help her move, but then Clair appeared at her bedroom door, wearing a solemn expression. "Jared's here," she announced.

seventeen

As Clair retreated from her bedroom, Kori glanced down at the wedding band on her finger. It was as conspicuous as five one stars in the nighttime sky. She didn't dare confront Jared wearing it. Slipping it off, Kori set it in her jewelry case. Then, picking up the engagement ring, she put it in the pocket of her blue jeans, knowing she must return it, knowing the time was now.

She walked into the living room. "Hi, Jared. I didn't expect you back from deer hunting till tomorrow."

He opened his mouth to reply but seemed to think better of it. Then he continued to stand there in the little entry hall, hands inside his black, down ski vest. Beneath it, he wore a red plaid flannel shirt tucked into black jeans. Kori also noticed that he sported a new reddish-brown beard that contrasted nicely with his sandy-blond hair. He looked every bit the outdoorsman, the hunter.

"Why don't you come in?" Kori invited. "We can sit and talk." She looked askance at her roommates, hoping they'd take a hint and vacate the living room.

They did.

"I've got tons of letters to write," Dana blurted, heading for her bedroom.

"Oh, and I have bills to pay," Clair announced, taking her leave as well.

Forcing a little smile, Kori looked back at Jared.

"I've been gone a whole week and this is the kind of greeting I get?" he muttered, wearing a dubious expression.

Kori didn't know what to say, especially since Jared gave her no time to reply. He swiftly closed the distance between them, pulling her into a fierce embrace.

143

"I missed you," he said huskily, his whiskered chin pressing against her cheek.

Kori bit her lower lip. How could she respond?

When she didn't, Jared released her. "Get your coat. We're leaving."

"Jared, wait, I need to talk to you."

"We can talk on the way to Joe's house."

Kori frowned. "Joe's house?"

He nodded. "There's a college football game on TV this afternoon."

Kori smiled reluctantly. She had no intention of spending the afternoon watching football. Jared must have read her thoughts and in one quick move, he opened the closet door, grabbing Kori's coat. Then he opened the door to the apartment.

"C'mon, let's go."

She sighed in resignation. She didn't want to break their engagement in Jared's truck, but if she must, so be it. "Let me get my purse."

"You don't need your purse."

"Jared!"

He took ahold of Kori's elbow and propelled her out of the apartment. Then he slammed the door behind them. In the hallway, he helped her on with her coat, but never slowed his pace.

"What's the rush?" Kori asked irritably. She was irked that she didn't have her keys. When she returned, she'd have to buzz up to the apartment and ask Clair or Dana to let her in. She hoped they didn't have plans this afternoon, but then again, maybe this wouldn't take long. "Jared, slow down."

"I hate missing the kickoff, you know that!"

Kori rolled her eyes, but buttoned up her coat nevertheless. "We have to talk, Jared," she fairly pleaded. "*Before* kickoff."

"I told you we'll talk on the way to Joe's house."

"Who's Joe?" Kori asked as they entered the elevator.

"A friend from Racine."

"Racine? But that's about a forty-five minute drive from here."

He glowered at her. "Plenty of time to talk, huh?"

The elevator doors opened, and walking through the lobby, they left the apartment complex. Through the freezing rain and gloom of the day, Kori did a quick scan of the parking lot, but she didn't see Brent's truck anywhere. Too bad, since she might have been able to forestall Jared long enough for Brent to join them in the talking.

Jared opened the door, saw her into his aging pickup, and then walked around to the other side where he climbed up into the driver's seat. Kori watched him, noticing for the first time that he looked. . .angry?

Kori strapped on her seat belt. "Jared—"

"Not yet."

He pulled out of the parking lot with tires squealing and then sped down the icy street toward the expressway.

"What's wrong, Jared?" Kori asked. He was never one to drive like a maniac. . .until now.

"What do you think is wrong?" he shot at her. "My best girl doesn't show up at the party last night, making me look like a fool. I was going to surprise you, Kori. I came back from hunting early just to surprise you."

"I heard. Dana told me and I'm sorry."

"You're sorry? How sorry are you, Kori?"

"I. . .I don't know what you mean. . ."

"Yeah? Well, let me clarify it for you. First, I felt like a fool, but then I got worried. I left the tavern and headed for your apartment to find out what happened to you. Dana told me your car broke down and that you were with some other friends—friends with a car, make that a utility vehicle. And you must have really been grateful for the ride," Jared drawled sarcastically, "because you gave the driver a good, long kiss."

Kori felt the blood drain from her face.

"I waited around and saw the whole thing," Jared muttered furiously, "so don't deny it!"

"I won't."

He glared at her, wearing an expression of incredulity.

"That's what I have to talk to you about," Kori persisted. "You saw me last night with Brent. . .my husband. Brent and I . . .well, we've decided to give our marriage another chance."

In reply, he stomped on the accelerator.

"Jared!" she screamed. "Slow down!"

Much to her relief, he did except his white-knuckled grip on the steering wheel caused Kori yet another measure of alarm. He was in a rage and driving seventy miles an hour on a slippery road.

"I didn't want to tell you like this," she said ruefully, hoping he'd relax and want to at least discuss the matter.

But Jared didn't reply, nor did he relax.

"Please," she begged. "Turn around and take me home."

Again, no reply as the pickup continued to fly down the freeway, faster than the law allowed.

Kori never knew such fear. Jared careened in and out of traffic, randomly changing lanes and cutting in front of other automobiles. Horns blared from under the palms of offended drivers, until at last he exited the freeway, forcing an audible sigh of relief from Kori. Her relief was, however, short-lived. Turning left at the stoplight, he then began to speed down Highway 20, toward the small city of Racine.

る

Brent stopped pacing and looked at his wristwatch. "Okay, now she's been gone for over an hour." He glanced at Clair, then Dana, and resumed his pacing. "How long does it take to say: *our engagement is over, I'm going back to my husband?*"

Clair chuckled. "Take it easy, Brent. Kori's not exactly heartless, you know. She's probably trying to break it to Jared nice and slow."

"She should have waited for me."

"I don't think Jared gave her much of a choice. They were gone in a flash."

Dana nodded. "Kori didn't even take her purse."

"More's the reason I'm worried. And I don't like the

thought of my wife alone with that guy."

"Don't you trust her?" Dana asked.

"Of course I trust her!" Brent declared as he momentarily ceased his pacing. "It's him I don't trust. I'm worried about Kori's welfare. I don't know what Jared is capable of when faced with rejection by the woman he says he loves. All I know is that a good percentage of the assaults I treat in the ER are related to crimes of passion."

"No kidding?" Dana shook her head, amazed. "I wonder if Jared is capable of committing a crime of passion."

"He's not," Clair stated emphatically.

"How do you know?" Brent challenged her. "Look, Clair, anyone is capable of anything, given the right circumstance." He resumed his pacing. "Kori mentioned that Jared's got a fridge full of beer, so it's likely he'd have an explosive nature if he were intoxicated."

"Good point, Brent," Dana said, looking concerned.

"Will you two stop it? Kori has only been gone an hour!" Clair exclaimed, throwing her hands in the air, looking exasperated. "And that includes drive time. How intoxicated can you get in an hour?" She crossed the room and turned on the television. "Stop your worrying, Dana, and, Brent, sit down and stop that pacing. You're making me nervous. Kori's fine. She'll probably be walking in any minute now."

Taking a seat in one of the armchairs, Brent looked at his watch once more. "I hope you're right, Clair," he muttered. "I hope you're right."

eighteen

"This one's for you, Kori," Jared said, pulling another beer out of Joe's refrigerator. It was his umpteenth—Kori had lost count long ago. "To the love of my life," he continued in a mock toast, popping off the top. "To the only woman I ever thought highly enough of to ask her to be my wife."

Standing in the corner of the kitchen, Kori grimaced. Jared seemed so hurt and she felt awful about it. However, nothing she said seemed to eased his pain, so he chose to drown his sorrows in beer.

Jared's friends were in the den, watching the game on TV, and Kori found herself wishing—no, praying that Jared would join them so she could sneak in a phone call for help.

"I can't believe you're dumping me for him," Jared lamented. Turning, he walked toward Kori until he stood just inches away. "What's he got that I don't?"

Her heart ached for at least the seventh time since they'd arrived here over two hours ago. "Jared, don't do this. . .I've tried to explain."

"What's he got, Kori?" he demanded, angrily now.

"My heart!" she finally cried. "Brent's got my heart."

Jared pulled his bearded chin back, frowning as he considered her statement. Finally he shook his head. "That makes no sense, Kori. That makes no sense at all!"

"Hey, Jare," his buddy, Craig, said, coming into the kitchen. "You're missing the game."

"I don't care," he groused, draining his beer.

Puzzled, Craig looked over at Kori, then back at Jared. "Lover's quarrel going on here?"

"Something like that," he replied gruffly.

Craig gave each of them another look before trying to

148

change the subject. He glanced at Kori. "Joe and I would have told the girls to put off their shopping trip until you arrived," he said apologetically, "but we didn't know Jared was going to bring you along this afternoon."

"That's okay. Don't worry about it."

Jared pulled another beer from the fridge. "Kori and I will be along shortly," he told his friend, swaying slightly.

"All right, all right. I can take a hint." Craig pulled a beer out for himself and left the kitchen for the football game and the four other rowdy men watching it.

Kori folded her arms in front of her. After being around Brent's friends she'd come to realize just how much she abhorred the drinking and carrying on that was so typical of Jared and "the guys." Didn't they understand that they could have fun without the beer? Kori had thought yesterday was one of the most enjoyable days of her life and not one alcoholic beverage had been served.

"There's no way that guy loves you more than I do," Jared slurred in self-pity. But then a whoop from the other room caught his attention and he sauntered out of the kitchen.

Watching him go, Kori couldn't help breathing a sigh of relief. She waited a moment to be sure Jared was thoroughly preoccupied before heading for the wall-mounted telephone on the other side of the kitchen. She dialed home and Clair answered.

"Where are you? Brent is about to have a nervous breakdown over here."

"Listen, Clair, I just have a moment. Jared is drinking. Heavily. I told him about Brent and me, but he's not taking the news very well. Can you come and get me?"

"Sure. Where are you?"

"In Racine."

"Racine?"

"Yes. I'll explain later."

"I'll need directions."

"I've got them. Ready? Take I-94 and exit on Highway 20.

Take that all the way through town and turn on Taylor. There's a park across the street. I'll be waiting right on the corner."

"The weather's bad," Clair informed her. "It'll take me about an hour."

"Fine. Jared should be passed out by then—I hope."

"Oh, Kori. . ."

Brent took the phone. "Kori, are you all right?"

"Yes. But I need to hang up. Jared will be even more angry if he finds me on the phone."

"I'm coming with Clair."

"Good." A kind of peace flowed through Kori knowing Brent was on his way. "I'll see you in awhile."

She hung up the telephone just as Jared entered the kitchen. Hoping to cover her actions, she ripped open a bag of potato chips that had been on the counter under the phone.

"I was just coming to get those," Jared muttered.

"Let me put them into a bowl for you."

He shook his head at her. "No bowl, Kori. We'll just eat them out of the bag." Jared's intoxicated gaze lingered on her face. "Always thinking fancy, aren't you?" His voice had softened. "You like the cheese and sausage all cut up real pretty and the potato chips in a bowl." He swallowed, narrowing his gaze. "You're probably the best thing that ever happened to me."

Guilt rose up in Kori, threatening to suffocate her. She wanted to say something profound—something that would penetrate his drunken haze, soothe his heart, and set her free, all at the same time. But no words would come.

"You told me you were getting a divorce."

"Jared, I've tried to explain. After seeing Brent," she said carefully, "and after thinking it over, I. . .I changed my mind."

Jared cursed and slammed down his empty beer can, causing Kori to flinch. "How can you change your mind after saying you'd marry me?"

How could I change my mind. . .? The words echoed in Kori's head. Wasn't that the very thing of which she'd accused Brent? Changing his mind?

Craig entered the kitchen then, with Joe right behind him. "Okay, break it up. Fighters to their corners."

His friends chuckled, but Jared was not amused. He grabbed the potato chips from Kori, another beer, and walked out of the room. His friends opened the refrigerator, pulled out more beer, and then they too left the kitchen.

Alone once more, Kori couldn't help but see the sad irony of her situation. She had hated the heartbreak Brent imposed upon her when he said he didn't love her anymore, and here she was inflicting a similar pain on Jared. She had never wanted to hurt him; she only wanted to do the right thing and giving her marriage another chance was the right thing to do. She was certain of at least that much.

Jesus, she whispered in prayer, *this situation is too overwhelming for me. Would You please take care of it. . .so I can someday stand up in church and give one of those testimonies of faith? Jesus, I'm depending on You. . .*

એ

Brent insisted that he and Clair take his truck while Dana agreed to stay at the apartment in case Kori called back. "I've got my cell phone," he told her as they left. "You've got the number."

"I'll call if I hear anything," Dana promised.

The roads were sleet-covered and the freezing rain continued to fall. "I'm glad we took your vehicle," Clair said as they drove past a car that had slid off the road. A police car and tow truck were already on the scene.

"This four-wheel drive comes in handy," Brent replied with a slight grin. "Even in California."

Clair was silent and seemed introspective as they continued their drive to Racine. Finally she turned to him and said, "Thanks, Brent."

"Thanks? For what?"

"For reconciling with Kori."

He chuckled. "I had no choice, Clair. I love my wife. . . even though it took me long enough to realize it."

"Then I guess that's what I'm thanking you for. . .for coming to your senses. I mean, what if Kori would have really married Jared?" Clair shook her head. "I just never thought they made a good match. He's too much into himself, always looking for a good time, and that would have bored Kori to death. She wants a home and kids and, even though she always said Jared is a stable man, he's obviously not a family man."

Brent glanced her way. "Clair, no one is stable when he's drunk, and I'm worried that Jared's 'good time' this afternoon could get someone killed. Especially if he decides to climb behind the wheel of a car. I mean, didn't you tell me that he's drinking heavily?"

Clair nodded. "That's what Kori said. But I still don't think he'd ever hurt anyone. Jared is basically a very nice, decent guy. Kori wouldn't have given him the time of day otherwise."

"Well, whatever he is," Brent replied, concentrating on the slippery road before him, "he's drunk now, and I want my wife as far away from him as possible."

❧

Kori looked at her wristwatch. It was nearly four o'clock. Brent and Clair should be waiting for her. Walking to the kitchen window, she peered out at the freezing rain that fell steadily. Because of the gloom of the day, it seemed dark outside already. Dark and wintery.

She let the curtain fall back into place. Then she cautiously made her way into the hallway. Less than a half hour ago, Jared had poured out his heart to his friends, who, of course, took his side. Now they weren't talking to Kori when they entered the kitchen to get their beers, whereas before they had at least attempted to be friendly. Even so, Jared had refused to let her go.

"You're staying with me, Kori," he had grumbled. He seemed to think that if he kept her here she'd somehow change her mind again, but if she left, she'd be out of his life forever. He was like a man trying to hang onto the wind.

Just outside the den now, Kori stole a glance at him. She sighed in relief at the sight of his sleeping figure, reclined on the couch. Finally! Moving quickly, but as quietly as possible, Kori entered the living room and found her coat. Putting it on, she touched the bulge in her blue jeans pocket. Jared's engagement ring.

She pulled it from her pocket and stared at it, wondering what to do. Should she leave it here for Jared to find? Stop by at his house another time when he wasn't drinking? Mail it?

No, she decided, *I have to settle this now. Any other way will only prolong the inevitable. It's over between Jared and me, but if I hang onto his ring that'll just give him an excuse to see me again.*

As she walked back through the house and rounded the corner to the den, Dave, another of Jared's friends, looked up from where he sat in a comfortable armchair. "Goin' somewhere?" he asked sarcastically.

Kori held her breath, looking at Jared, but much to her relief, he didn't awaken. Looking back at Dave, she nodded. "Yes, I'm leaving. I've arranged a ride home. But will you make sure Jared doesn't drive drunk?"

"Of course," he shot at her, his voice filled with animosity. "What kind of friend do you think I am?"

Kori didn't reply, but twirled the engagement ring in her palm nervously. She could hardly give it to Dave and expect he'd pass it along to Jared. Obviously, he wasn't going to do her any favors. She'd have to do it herself.

Stepping into the room filled with cigarette smoke and the stench of beer, Kori walked slowly toward the man she had intended to marry up until a few days ago. Relief mingled with sadness as she realized she would no longer be marrying a man she didn't love, yet she did have feelings for him. Dreams had been dashed this day, more his than hers, and Kori felt so sorry about hurting Jared.

She softly touched the rim of the pocket on his flannel shirt and then dropped the ring inside. Jared never stirred.

Turning on her heel then, Kori left the room. She practically ran through the house and to the front door. Touching the doorknob, she suddenly heard Jared calling her name. Like a rumble of thunder off in the distance, Kori was instantly aware of some sort of ominous doom.

"Don't you dare leave!" he roared.

Ignoring the command, she opened the door and fled. A thin layer of ice covered the front stairs and she nearly slipped. Her heart pounded as fear rose up inside her. She'd never be able to run from Jared in this weather. Why had he awakened? But Kori suspected the answer to that one; no doubt Dave had roused him.

Reaching the front sidewalk, Kori turned left and began to half run, half slide, making her way toward the highway where she prayed Brent was waiting for her.

"Kori!"

"Go back inside the house, Jared," she called over her shoulder. Looking back, she saw he was on the front porch stairs. Then, much to her horror, he jumped and fairly skied down the ice-covered lawn. All without falling! Now he was just behind her.

With a little gasp, Kori turned and did her best to run. She nearly slipped and fell several times, but managed to maintain her balance. Jared wasn't that fortunate. One quick glance behind her showed him sitting on his backside. He glared at her, looking furious, and Kori imagined that he was angry enough to kill. But would he? Never in her relationship with Jared had she seen him drunk like this. All she knew now was that she had to get away. He obviously wasn't in his right mind, and Kori was as scared as she'd ever been.

She neared the corner of Taylor and spotted Brent's truck, but she didn't slow her pace, even though she nearly slipped on the icy walk again. Behind her, Jared was calling her, threatening her. She was so frightened, she began to cry and her tears fused with the sleet raining down, soaking her hair, her face, her coat.

Reaching the highway, Kori saw Brent get out of his truck. Through the encroaching darkness, she saw him frown. She watched as Brent looked past her to Jared, who was gaining on her.

"No, Jesus," Kori muttered in prayer, "not a fight between Brent and Jared. Jared's drunk and he could hurt Brent. . .but he wouldn't mean it, I know he wouldn't."

"Kori, stop!"

Was that Brent—or Jared? Kori's heart was hammering so loudly in her ears, but she felt like she had to keep running.

"Kori!"

That time she was sure it was Brent who called her name. She noticed the sudden look of panic and horror that crossed his dark features and then, too late, she saw the oncoming car. Braking on the icy pavement, it veered out of control. It came straight for her.

Kori screamed.

nineteen

Brent met his sister-in-law in the noisy waiting room of the hospital.

"Well?" Clair asked anxiously. "How is she, Brent? What's going on?"

"Kori's going to be all right," he began. "But I was right, she's got a dislocated shoulder. And we might be looking at a hip and/or back injury. She's getting X rays right now."

Clair sat back in her chair and Brent saw her eyes fill with tears.

"She's going to be okay," he repeated.

"But I don't think I'll ever get the picture of Kori being hit by that car out of my mind," she said, sobbing softly.

"Me either," Brent muttered, handing Clair a box of Kleenex tissues from a neighboring table. Then he sat down in the chair beside her. "It all still seems so unreal."

"Kori must have been thrown ten feet," she sniffed.

"Yes, but we're lucky that stretch of highway going through town has a speed limit of thirty-five. The driver claims she was only going about twenty miles an hour because of the bad weather. Really, Kori is fortunate to be alive."

"But there was so much blood on her face, Brent."

"That was due to the laceration on her scalp. Head wounds bleed a lot. A few stitches and Kori will be as good as new. As for her shoulder, the nurses are giving her some pain medication now and as soon as she's relaxed, the physician will manipulate it back into place."

"It sounds awful. Poor, Kori. . .getting 'manipulated.' And Jared. . .what's going to happen to him?"

"He can rot in jail for all I care!"

Clair gasped, obviously surprised by his vehemence. "Do

156

you really think he'll get thrown in jail? I mean it isn't like he was driving drunk and hit Kori."

"It isn't? I happen to think it's very much the same," Brent said adamantly. He shifted his sitting position, running a hand through his hair. He knew his previous remark didn't sound very Christian-like, but his feelings for Jared Graham right now were not very Christian. Brent blamed him for Kori's accident and he had every intention of pressing charges. "I suppose the police will find him and question him. As for any imprisonment—well, I really don't know."

Clair nodded. "I just can't believe he ran from the scene."

Brent clenched his jaw, but he decided not to waste his energy on anger. Kori needed him now, whereas his dealings with Graham could wait. Then, for the first time since the accident, Brent suddenly felt uncomfortably cold and wet. His clothes were soaked from being out in the rain and tending to Kori until the ambulance arrived. Clair, too, was drenched.

"Listen," Brent said, leaning forward with elbows on his knees, "how about if you give Dana a call and ask her to bring you some dry clothes. I'm going to call Mark and request the same. . .and I'm hoping he knows Ryan Carlson's phone number. If Kori needs an orthopedic surgeon, I want a recommendation—"

"Oh, Brent. . .surgery?" More tears filled her eyes.

"It's a possibility. Now, go on," he encouraged her. "Call Dana." He sighed heavily then. "I have a feeling it's going to be a long night."

❧

Nearly two hours later, Kori lay relatively comfortably on the gurney in the emergency department's exam room. The laceration on her head had been sewn to Brent's satisfaction, her shoulder popped back into place. The pain medication was making her body feel light and relaxed and, despite all that had happened, she could not mistake the peace that flowed inside her. Somehow she sensed that Jesus was taking care of everything, just as she'd asked.

"Kori?"

She turned her head and smiled weakly at Brent who was leaning over the side of the gurney.

"How are you feeling?"

"Can't say this has been the best day I ever had," she admitted, "but I'm fine."

He grinned, looking amused. "Fine, huh? That's not what your X rays show."

"And what do they show, Dr. McDonald?" Kori asked tartly.

"Well, according to the films, *Mrs. McDonald,*" he retorted, "you've got a fractured hip."

Kori grimaced. "How bad?"

"Bad enough to warrant surgery, I'm afraid. I'm waiting for Ryan. He's agreed to come down to the hospital and recommend an orthopedist for us." Brent shook his head. "I feel so helpless because I don't know any of these guys."

"Who's the orthopedist on call?" Kori wanted to know. "I work with a lot of them when Ryan refers his patients out."

"Ever hear of Dr. Alfred Morris?"

Kori managed a nod. "He's with a reputable physicians' group. I'm sure he's fine."

"Well, I don't want 'fine' operating on you, Kori. I want the best."

She smiled up at him. "You're so sweet, Brent."

"And you're about the best patient I've ever known," he teased her. "I wish all of my patients were like you. No moaning and groaning. No persistent demands."

"Why should I moan and groan and make demands," she teased him back, "when I have you to do that for me?"

Brent laughed. "Yeah, I suppose you've got a point there." Leaning over the guard-rail on the bed, he kissed her gently, reverently. Straightening, he said, "Clair isn't taking any of this very well at all."

"Clair?" Kori frowned. "But she's always levelheaded."

"This evening, she's near hysteria. She can't stop crying."

"Clair?"

Brent nodded. "I thought maybe I'd leave for awhile and change clothes so she can come in and visit with you. This hospital has a rule that only one guest can be in a patient's exam room."

Kori nodded. "All right."

"Dana's out in the waiting area and she brought Clair some dry clothes. Mark and Julia are out there too, and Mark has clothes for me. Now we're just waiting on Ryan."

"What about Jared?"

Brent's shadowy gaze seemed to blacken in fury. "What about him?"

"I. . .well, I just wondered. . ." Kori was suddenly intimidated to ask further, given her husband's seething expression.

"What are you wondering, Kori?" Brent asked darkly. "Are you wondering if he stayed around at the accident site to make sure you were okay? Are you wondering if he came to the hospital, concerned over your welfare? Well, the answer to those questions is no!"

With her uninjured arm, she reached up and laid her palm gently against Brent's cheek, caressing it. "I love you, Brent," she whispered. "I'm so sure of it now. But please, don't be angry with Jared. He was hurt and—"

"I don't want to talk about him," Brent said resolutely. Then, taking hold of her hand, he placed a firm kiss on her fingers. "And I love you, too. But I never want to hear you mention the name Jared Graham again," he warned her. "Ever! Is that clear?"

Kori nodded, deciding that she was in no position to argue.

"All right then, I'm going to send Clair in, and when Ryan gets here, I'll come back."

After one last kiss, Brent left the exam room, leaving Kori to ponder over his reaction. True, Jared's actions were a factor in the accident. But it wasn't Jared's fault. Kori could hardly blame him when it was she, herself, who hadn't been watching where she was going. Surely, Brent had to know that, too. Then why was he being so hostile at the mere mention of

Jared's name? Weren't Christians supposed to "love" everyone? Wasn't that what following Jesus was all about?

Minutes later, Clair walked in. Her face was tear-streaked, confirming everything Brent had said. She tried to smile. "How are you feeling, Kori? Are you in any pain?"

"A little, but it's nothing compared to what I experienced earlier."

"Oh, Kori. . ." Clair's voice sounded broken.

"Don't cry, Sis. I'm really okay."

Through her tear-sparkling eyes, Clair managed to give her a skeptical look. "Did Brent tell you that your hip is broken and you're going to have surgery? You are hardly okay."

"Yes, he told me."

"And?"

Kori lifted a brow, not understanding Clair's meaning.

"Aren't you scared? Oh, of course you must be! I'm sorry. It's just that. . .I'm so scared." More tears pooled in Clair's eyes, spilling onto her cheeks.

Kori reached out to her. "I'm not afraid of having surgery, if that's what you mean. Why are you scared?"

Clair took her hand. "Because. . .well, anything could go wrong and I. . .I just don't want to lose you, Kori. You're my little sister. You're my best friend. Stuff like this isn't supposed to happen to people like us. We're good people. This doesn't seem fair."

Squeezing her sister's hand with as much strength as she could muster, Kori gently replied, "Let me see if I can explain something to you. Yesterday, Thanksgiving Day, was really that for me for the first time in my life. I realized that I have so much to be thankful for. I was reconciled to Brent, the man I've always loved—even after our two and a half year separation, even after trying to make myself believe I wanted to marry Jared. And yesterday was also a special day for me because. . .well, because I became a Christian."

Clair suddenly had clouds of questions in her eyes. "A Christian?"

Kori nodded. "One of those crazy born-again people I've been rolling my eyes at ever since I met Ryan Carlson." She chuckled softly. "I started thinking about it and realized that Jesus Christ is my only guarantee in this life. His promises are recorded in the Bible and the peace I'm feeling now is from Him. And that's why I'm not scared, Clair. I have Christ."

"Some God He is to let you get hit by a car," she answered, pulling her hand free and wiping away an errant tear.

"But better me, Clair, than Brent or Jared. . .or you. How would I have ever lived with myself if someone else got hurt because of me?" Kori shook her head. "I wouldn't have been able to stand it. Jesus knew that about me. That's why He let this accident happen—*to me.*"

"You're not making sense."

Kori sighed as a wave of weariness swept over her. "Maybe not, but I just know that this is His way and it's the best way and. . .I'm going to be just fine. It's something I feel in my heart."

With a cluck of her tongue, Clair replied, "I think you're talking out of your head because of the pain medication."

Kori did her best to shake her head to the contrary. "I mean what I said."

Clair shrugged.

"Ryan tried to tell me for years about Christ," she went on reflectively, "but I wouldn't listen. It was only when Brent came back that I wanted to hear—because I wanted to understand the change in him. Now I know. And now I've got it for myself."

"The guarantee you always wanted."

"Yes. And a love to last forever. God's love."

Clair moved the corner chair closer to Kori's bedside. Then she sat down. "You know," she said at last, "I feel better. I think your peace might be rubbing off on me."

Kori smiled, but suddenly she was so tired she couldn't stay awake another moment. Closing her eyes, she fell into a deep, peaceful sleep.

twenty

As Brent had predicted, the night was indeed long. Ryan arrived at the hospital and, after much discussion, it was decided that Kori would be transferred to another medical facility and admitted under the care of a highly acclaimed orthopedic surgeon. Once the relocation had been completed, Kori was scheduled for surgery first thing Saturday.

That morning, Brent sat in the family waiting area after a brief meeting with the anesthesiologist. He had been allowed to stay by Kori's side right up until they wheeled her off to the operating room. Looking into his coffee cup now, he found himself thinking about all the dangers of general anesthesia and all the risks involved with surgery.

"Quit worrying," Mark told him in an amused tone of voice.

Brent glanced at his friend, sitting beside him. He was grateful that Mark had offered to pray with him and keep him company this morning. He grinned challengingly. "How do you know I'm worrying?"

Mark folded the business section of the newspaper and set it in his lap. "I can see it in your face. You've got great big worry lines across your forehead."

"Those aren't worry lines. I was just frowning because something's floating in my coffee."

"Sure, and now you're fibbing on top of it."

Brent chuckled lightly.

"You're not really worried, are you, Brent?" Clair asked seriously. She sat just across from them. "You said this was all standard procedure for someone in Kori's condition."

Taking one look at his sister-in-law's concerned expression, he decided he'd better not fret, if for no other reason than to keep Clair calm. He smiled. "I'm just tired, that's all." And that was the truth, too!

She gave a short laugh. "Well, that's to be expected. You haven't slept all night. At least I got to go home and get a decent amount of sleep."

"I'll survive," he replied. "I've done enough double shifts at the hospital that I should be used to it by now."

"Hope you're planning to go home for awhile and get some rest after Kori comes out of surgery," Mark said in a tone of friendly advice.

Brent nodded. As much as he hated the thought of leaving Kori, he knew his limit and it was getting close.

"Yeah, I have to get some sleep," he muttered, catching the shadow of a man entering the waiting area. Looking up curiously, his full gaze rested upon none other than Jared Graham. At first, Brent was so surprised, he thought he was seeing things. It seemed too incredible. Him? Here? Of all the nerve! But, as the guy headed toward them, he knew this wasn't a product of weary imaginings.

"What are you doing here?" he fairly spat, standing so abruptly that his coffee sloshed over the edge of the cup.

Mark stood as well. "Easy, Brent," he said in soft warning, placing a hand on his friend's shoulder.

Brent shrugged it off. "You have no business here, Graham, so leave."

By now, Clair was standing also. Her wary gaze shifted between Brent and Jared, finally coming to rest on Brent. "I said it was okay for him to come," she admitted at last.

"What?"

"He phoned me late last night," Clair quickly explained. "Jared is as concerned about Kori as we are."

"Oh, right," Brent replied sarcastically, his gaze never wavering from Jared's expressionless, bearded face. "And that's why he fled the accident scene. . .because he was so concerned about her."

The man's green eyes darkened with suppressed emotion, a mixture, it seemed, of guilt and fury. Yet Brent stood undaunted. "I want you out of here, Graham. Now."

"Brent, please, give him a chance," Clair pleaded. "Jared knows what he did was wrong, but—"

"But nothing." Brent turned to his sister-in-law. "He either leaves on his own, or I call the hospital's security staff. In fact, I'm sure the police would love to know where he is."

A pained look crossed Clair's features, confusing Brent. Whose side was she on, anyhow? How could she be concerned for her sister's welfare and feel sorry for the person who caused her accident?

"I'll leave, Clair," Jared said, breaking his tight-lipped silence. "I told you he'd be unreasonable." After a scathing glance at Brent, he turned and left the waiting room.

Satisfied with the outcome, Brent sat back down in his chair. Mark slowly followed suit; however, Clair just stood there, glaring at her brother-in-law.

"I thought you, a Christian, were all about love and forgiveness," she shot at him. "That's what you expected from Kori, wasn't it? Forgiveness? And love? Isn't that what you made her believe—that love conquers all? I almost believed it, too, but obviously your faith is nothing but a pack of lies!"

Brent stood again. "Clair, I—"

"No! You never even gave Jared a chance," she railed. "I listened to him pour his heart out for over an hour last night. He's feeling terrible about causing Kori's accident. Even she said it's not entirely his fault."

"And what about his disappearing act after Kori was struck by that car? Did he tell you he feels really bad about that, too?" Brent asked, sarcasm dripping from every word.

"Yes, as a matter of fact, he did." Clair paused, lifting her chin defiantly. Under different circumstances, Brent might have grinned, since it was an expression he'd seen on Kori any number of times. But now, the woman standing before him was advocating for a man Brent thought he might even hate.

"He was scared," Clair said. "Jared thought he'd killed Kori. He was beside himself, wondering, worrying, and knowing nothing. He said he tried calling several local hospitals, but no one would give him any information. Then the police came to Jared's door and told him that Kori was hospitalized and in satisfactory condition. He said they questioned him, but that's all, but for the next several hours Jared said he considered his whole life, where he'd been, where he was going. He did a thorough self-examination and got in touch with his inner being."

Brent rolled his eyes. "Save your breath, Clair. I am unimpressed with pseudopsychology. It's a useless bunch of nonsense in my opinion."

"Well, no matter. My point is this: Jared needs to heal emotionally. He told me he was hurt that Kori broke their engagement, but he admitted he was wrong to get drunk. But, Brent," Clair said beseechingly now, "doesn't Jared deserve the chance to know that Kori is going to be all right and then attempt to apologize to her?"

"No!" he declared hotly.

Clair threw her hands in the air, looking disgusted.

"Listen," Mark said objectively, "she's got a point, Brent. Remember the Scriptures say we need to love our enemies and forgive one another even as God for Christ's sake has forgiven us."

"Spare me the sermon," Brent replied peevishly.

"Good. Then you remember." A wry grin split Mark's face. "So how about I go try and catch up to Jared? We can, at least, invite him to sit here and wait out the surgery with us. Once he knows Kori is fine, he'll leave."

Brent gave his longtime friend an incredulous look, but sensed he was fighting a losing battle. Between Mark's Scripture whipping and Clair's gaze, throwing daggers at him, he didn't have a chance. "Yeah, sure, whatever. . ." he grumbled at last. "Go get him."

As Mark left the waiting area, Brent crossed the room and stood by the window. There, he had a perfect view of the wide expanse of Lake Michigan. It reminded him of the

Pacific Ocean and suddenly a wave of homesickness rushed through him. Oh! how he wished he and Kori could just up and leave this mess and start their lives together anew. He'd love to fly her home right away. If only he hadn't committed to be a groomsman in Mark's wedding.

"You're doing the right thing," Clair said, standing just behind him now.

Brent didn't even bother turning around.

"We all have certain chapters of our lives that have to be closed before we can go on living—and that's what you're allowing Jared to do."

Brent wanted to say that Jared could have closed this particular chapter of his life days ago if he hadn't gone ballistic over Kori's decision; however, he swallowed the reply, praying the bitter taste in his mouth would go down along with it.

Mark returned about a half hour later, Jared Graham in tow. Each carried a cup of steaming coffee. Brent remained at the window, doing his best to ignore the small talk that ensued after they took a seat.

"Come and join us, Brent," Clair called to him.

"No, thanks," he muttered grouchily. And he stood there for what seemed like an interminable time, only leaving once when he walked down the hallway to purchase a diet cola from out of the vending machine.

At long last, the surgeon appeared. "Everything went very well," he announced. "No surprises." He then went on to explain how he and his staff had pinned Kori's hip and repaired several minor fractures. "It was similar to putting a broken dish back together."

Out of the corner of his eye, Brent saw Clair sway slightly. He took hold of her elbow in an attempt to steady her.

"Oh, poor Kori," she said, tears pooling in her eyes. "Her hip was like a broken dish. . .?"

"Not to worry," the surgeon replied lightly, waving off the remark. "We'll have her dancing down the hospital corridors in no time. Your sister is going to be as good as new." Turning to Brent, he added, "She will, of course, require physical therapy, but nothing extensive. I expect her to make a complete recovery."

Brent managed a small smile. "Good."

"For the immediate prognoses, she'll be in recovery for awhile and then taken back up to her room. The nurses will probably get her up this evening and in a few days, she can go home."

"Really?" Clair brightened hearing that.

After a few more exchanges, the surgeon took his leave. Brent turned to Jared, hoping he'd take his as well. However, the look of relief on the other man's face gave him pause, and Brent suddenly wondered if everything Clair had said was true. Jared really seemed concerned about Kori and, moreover, he looked quite penitent. But Brent was too exhausted to be amicable at the moment.

"I'm going back to the apartment to get some sleep," he muttered. "Thanks for coming. . .all of you. . ."

With a fleeting glance in Jared's direction, he walked out of the waiting room.

❧

Two days later, the nurse helped Kori back into bed after another walk around the hospital wing. Kori was finally getting used to the crutches, though her shoulder ached terribly at having to use them. Sometimes she didn't know which hurt more, her shoulder or her hip, not to mention the awful muscle aches and bruises that still covered much of her body. But in spite of her physical aches and pains, Kori still sensed that sweet peace and comforting presence of her Savior.

"There now, Mrs. McDonald," the young nurse said politely. "You can rest now and I heard the doctor say you'd be discharged later."

Kori smiled, nodding. He'd told her the same thing on his rounds that morning. She could go home today! She had phoned Brent earlier to share the good news, and he'd said that all of her belongings were now moved into his apartment.

He had also picked up her new car. The plan was they'd stay through the Christmas holiday here in Wisconsin, and by January, Kori would be healed enough to make the drive back to California with her "little red wagon" in tow. Both he and Kori's doctor expected her to make a rapid recovery, yet there were times when Kori couldn't imagine her body healing so fast.

"One step at a time," Brent had told her and that's about as far ahead as Kori could think for now.

The nurse left the room while Kori adjusted her hospital bed so she'd recline more comfortably. Sitting straight up was still terribly uncomfortable and she could only tolerate it for short intervals, while lying flat on her back caused her shoulder to throb.

As Kori finished getting herself situated, a knock sounded at the door. Before she could even reply, Jared poked his head into the room.

"Can I come in?"

Kori hesitated a moment, fearing that Brent would show up and discover Jared visiting with her. Although he had seemed less hostile toward Jared, Kori didn't want there to be any chance for a confrontation between the two men.

"I'll only stay a minute," Jared promised, as if to sway her decision.

At last she waved him into the room.

"I'm glad to see you're doing okay," he said, looking uncertain as he walked into the room. "Clair has kept me up on your progress."

Kori nodded for lack of a better reply. She suddenly wished she were still on her crutches so she could stand and talk to Jared. She felt so vulnerable like this.

He came up to her and stood beside the bed, his hand on the side rail. He shook his head and grinned. "I practiced a big long speech on the way over," he said, "and now I can't think of a single thing to say."

Kori managed a weak smile. The sight of Jared evoked so

many emotions in her. Maybe a small part of her had loved him after all. "Could I say something?"

He nodded.

"I've been doing a lot of thinking these past couple of days and. . .well, I can't change anything that's happened, but I can ask for your forgiveness. Will you forgive me, Jared?"

"What are you talking about?" he asked with a shaken expression. "Me forgive you? For what?"

Kori swallowed hard. "For hurting you."

Jared lowered himself so that his forearms now rested on the side rail. "You're crazy, you know that?"

She grinned slightly, for Jared's tone was affectionate despite his hard words.

"You? Hurt me?" He shook his head in wonder. "Look what I did to you. I nearly killed you, Kori, and you're asking for my forgiveness? I came here today to apologize to you!"

Her grin grew into a full-fledged smile. "Apology accepted. I forgive you."

Jared narrowed his gaze. "Just like that, huh?"

"Just like that."

"Man, Kori, you're a pushover." Jared straightened as a trace of bitterness entered his voice. "And your husband must have known it, too. All he had to do was apologize and you took him right back with little or no thought for us. . .me."

"That's not true, Jared."

He turned and walked to the window, standing with his back to her. Kori sighed, wishing there was something she could say that would make him finally understand.

"I thought I was over him, Jared," she stated honestly. "I thought I was free to love and marry you. But when Brent walked back into my life, I realized that wasn't the case. Not only were we still married, but I was still in love with him. I didn't plan it, nor did I intentionally deceive you. It's just something that happened."

"Yeah, I know," he replied, surprising Kori. He turned and leaned against the windowsill, his arms folded across his chest. "I know you're telling me the truth, but. . ." He paused, taking a deep breath. "But it hurts so bad, Kori, that I don't think I'll ever get over it."

Tears stung the backs of her eyes.

"And look at you. You're about as banged up as anyone I've ever seen. We're two people who were supposed to be in love, but now we've got wounds to last the rest of our lives!"

A fat tear slid down Kori's cheek as she realized she'd never heard Jared talk this way before. Deep, sharing his heart with her. "We'll heal, Jared," she promised, weeping openly now.

"Oh, don't do that," he said, rushing to her side. He handed her the box of tissues on the bedside table. "You know what's going to happen here, don't you? That husband of yours is going to walk in and hit the ceiling when he finds out I made you cry."

Kori chuckled through her tears. "Brent is going to hit the ceiling if he finds you here, period!"

Jared nodded. "It was a chance I had to take," he replied, looking more earnest than Kori had ever known. "I just had to see you one last time. I've got to know you're going to be happy with. . .with him."

"I'm going to be happy," Kori sniffed, wiping her tears away.

"Yeah, you look real happy," Jared retorted, a teasing light in his eyes. It was short-lived, however, and then his face took on a more intent, more determined, expression. Leaning over the bed, Jared suddenly pressed a firm kiss on her lips. "Good-bye, Kori," he whispered against her mouth. Straightening again, he lightly brushed the knuckles of his right hand against her cheek.

"Good-bye, Jared."

In the next moment, he turned and headed for the door, but stopped suddenly. Kori's gaze followed him, only to see Brent standing there, arms akimbo with a smoldering look in his eyes.

Oh, no! Kori thought as a sinking feeling enveloped her.

She closed her eyes, afraid to see what was coming next.

"Don't worry, pal," she heard Jared say. "That was good-bye forever, so don't even think about getting bent out of shape."

Not until she heard the door close did she look up. Jared was gone, but Brent still stood there, statue-still.

"Brent, I—"

"No, no. I don't want any explanations," he said, putting up a hand as he made his way slowly to her side. He put down the guardrail and then sat on the edge of the bed. "Just answer me yes or no. Was that really good-bye forever, Kori?"

"Yes," she replied in all honesty.

Pursing his lips, Brent momentarily thought it over. "Okay," he said at last. "I can live with that."

Kori felt like she would faint with relief, but when she looked back at Brent, he wore a little smirk on his face. But she didn't ask what he found so amusing, she just clung to him with all her might after he pulled her into a loving embrace.

"Ready to go home?" he asked, stroking her hair in long, soothing motions.

"Yes," she replied, tightening her hold around his neck. "Take me home."

epilogue

Eighteen Months Later

The sun was just beginning to set in the smoggy Los Angeles sky when Korah Mae McDonald climbed out of her red station wagon and walked toward the looming medical complex. Entering the lobby, she waved to Delores who sat at the Information Center and then headed for the Emergency Room.

"Well, hello, little mama," Sharon, one of the nurses, said. She was blond, middle-aged and extremely competent—or so Kori had heard. "Looking for Brent?"

She nodded. "Is he with a patient?"

"Nope. He's in back trying to eat supper and catch up on paperwork. If he's not careful, he'll end up eating an insurance form and signing his hamburger bun." Sharon laughed.

Kori smiled, and nodding her thanks, she made her way down the outer hallway toward the office that all the ER physicians shared while on duty.

"Oh, by the way," Sharon called after her. "How are you feeling?"

"Great. . .for a whale."

The nurse chuckled. "Have that ultrasound yet?"

"This afternoon." Kori held up the large cardboard envelope she'd been carrying. "Got 'em right here."

"And?" Sharon's eyes widened curiously.

She laughed nervously. "And I'll let Brent inform you of the results. . .right after I inform him." Kori didn't add that she'd been fretting over his reaction, praying he'd be delighted. . . once the shock wore off.

"Twins?"

"I'm not saying, Sharon," she stated, doing her best to be

adamant when she was fairly bursting to share the news with someone. "But it's not twins. I'll tell you that much."

The older woman frowned. "You're kidding? But I thought—"

"We were all wrong."

Sharon groaned. "And you're not going to set me straight? The wait's going to kill me!"

Kori pitched another smile as she turned and walked away. Chatting any longer and she'd spill the whole pot of beans! But she simply had to tell Brent first. He could be the one to tell his coworkers.

Rounding the corner, Kori paused at the office door. She could see Brent sitting in the far corner of the room, tapping a black pen against the desktop, staring blindly at his paperwork. Kori immediately knew he was concerned to the point of distraction and her heart went out to him.

As if sensing her presence, he looked up from his stack of forms. "Kori!" Dropping his pen, he stood and strode quickly toward her. "I've been waiting to hear from you," he said before placing a kiss on her lips. With hands upon her shoulders, he brought his chin back, scrutinizing her face. "So? What did your doctor say?"

"She said I'm not carrying twins, for one thing."

"You're not?" Brent narrowed his dark gaze. "But I heard the two heartbeats myself."

"Your diagnosis was incorrect, Dr. McDonald," Kori quipped, batting her lashes in feigned superiority.

"Oh, yeah? So what *is* the diagnosis?" Brent did not look amused and Kori immediately apologized for teasing him.

"Kori. . ."

"We're having triplets," she blurted.

"What?"

"It's true. Want to see the films?"

Nodding, Brent took them and walked toward the viewing box, mounted on the wall beside the desk. He switched on the light, snapped the X rays into place and considered them thoughtfully. At last, he turned slowly back around, wearing a broad grin. "We sure are having triplets!"

Kori returned the smile as gratitude filled her soul. While she'd known Brent wouldn't be angry at the news, she had wanted him to be just as excited as she was. From his expression, Kori realized her prayers had been answered.

"Let's see," Brent began, looking at the ceiling contemplatively, "we can get your mom to come for the first month and my mom can help with those two A.M. feedings whenever I have to work the night shift."

Kori laughed. "Clair will come and help. And Dana, too."

"I'll bet Juli wouldn't mind lending a hand for a week or so, especially if Mark gets that contract in San Diego."

"Oh, I don't know," Kori replied skeptically. "Julia's baby is due around the same time ours is—I mean the same time ours *are.*"

"Whew!" Brent said, running a hand through his hair. "Three babies. All at once." He suddenly beamed. "Praise the Lord!"

Kori nodded. They'd been praying for a baby for so long and the Lord saw fit to bless them with three! "God is certainly able to do exceeding, abundantly, and above all we ask."

"And think!" Brent added, pulling Kori into an embrace despite her protruding midsection. His eyes darkened passionately. "I love you."

With her arms around his neck, Kori murmured, "I love you, too."

"Ah-hem," came the female voice from the doorway. Brent looked up and Kori turned to find Sharon standing there. "You going to share the news about your wife's ultrasound, Brent, or keep it to yourself while the rest of us die from curiosity?"

He chuckled. "No one dies in *my* ER!" Then, taking Kori's hand, he led her toward the door. "I guess it's announcement time."

As she walked beside her husband to the nurse's station, an indescribable joy permeated Kori's being. This wasn't another impossible dream, this was reality! God's reality!

A Letter To Our Readers

Dear Reader:

In order that we might better contribute to your reading enjoyment, we would appreciate your taking a few minutes to respond to the following questions. When completed, please return to the following:

Rebecca Germany, Managing Editor
Heartsong Presents
PO Box 719
Uhrichsville, Ohio 44683

1. Did you enjoy reading *Second Time Around?*
   - ❏ Very much. I would like to see more books by this author!
   - ❏ Moderately
     I would have enjoyed it more if _____

     _____

2. Are you a member of **Heartsong Presents**? ❏ Yes ❏ No
   If no, where did you purchase this book? _____

   _____

3. What influenced your decision to purchase this book? (Check those that apply.)

❏ Cover	❏ Back cover copy
❏ Title	❏ Friends
❏ Publicity	❏ Other_____

4. How would you rate, on a scale from 1 (poor) to 5 (superior), the cover design? _____

5. On a scale from 1 (poor) to 10 (superior), please rate
   the following elements.

   ___Heroine   ___Plot

   ___Hero   ___Inspirational theme

   ___Setting   ___Secondary characters

6. What settings would you like to see covered in
   Heartsong Presents books?_____
   _____
   _____

7. What are some inspirational themes you would like
   to see treated in future books?_____
   _____
   _____

8. Would you be interested in reading other **Heartsong
   Presents** titles?   ❏ Yes   ❏ No

9. Please check your age range:
   ❏ Under 18   ❏ 18-24   ❏ 25-34
   ❏ 35-45   ❏ 46-55   ❏ Over 55

10. How many hours per week do you read? _____

Name _____
Occupation_____
Address_____
City_____ State_____ Zip _____